The Right Way to Do Wrong

The Right Way to Do Wrong

A Novel

BRAD INMAN

ISBN 978-1-947635-25-8 (Ebook Edition)

978-1-947635-26-5 (Paperback Edition)

Published by Inman Books

1

Three weeks before his interview at Moody's, the infamous bond credit rating agency, Baltazar Ponce, known to most as Baza, took the 6 train uptown to 200 Central Park South after finishing work at Mayor Bloomberg's office. It was a warm, sunny spring day and the sidewalks were alive with people enjoying a stroll in the balmy air. Baza was an immigrant from Honduras who had moved to the U.S. ten years previously to pursue an undergraduate education and found himself enjoying the rewards of working in the financial markets in New York in the early 2000s.

Baltazar Ponce, called "Baza" by all who knew him, was an immigrant more familiar with country clubs than with manual labor. Raised in a genteel and monied Honduras household, Baza was customarily fastidious in his ways. He was handsome in a baby-faced way, with a short nose and a dimple in his left cheek. Of aristocratic Spanish lineage, rather than Indian stock, he stood five feet six, taller than most men in Honduras, where the average height was only five feet two. He was lean and muscular from the countless hours he'd spent playing soccer since childhood. His blue eyes were a Central American anomaly, his hair the color of ripe dates.

As in most places with more bad weather than good, a day like this always brought New Yorkers out to the streets with friendlier smiles and better manners than usual. The men were in shirt-sleeves; the women wore flip-flops or strappy sandals with light, colorful dresses that caressed their bare legs as they walked. The buoyant mood inspired impulses that stayed buried in winter and wilted during the hot, humid days of summer.

Shortly after finishing his MBA at the NYU Stern School in 2002, Baza had scored the job in Mayor Bloomberg's New York City Housing Authority. Bloomberg, a billionaire regularly listed among the ten wealthiest people in America, was a life-long Democrat who registered Republican just before filing for the New York mayoral race. It was his first venture into electoral politics. He reportedly spent $50 million of his own money to win office in 2001.

For the mayor's office, Baza packaged mortgage revenue bonds that funded the development and maintenance of rental units under the City's affordable housing program. The City financed more than 20,000 units until the private market took over, in about 2000. Demand was so strong that developers rehabbed and built apartments as fast as the city could issue the permits. The trend was helped along by a rent control ordinance that favored private landlords and encouraged them to repair their property with municipal help.

Baza had met Bloomberg before. When he was 17 and touring colleges, his father had taken him to Dartmouth, with a side trip to New York City, where Baza senior was going to be interviewed by Bloomberg News for a feature on economic growth in Central America. Young Baza was enthralled by the seething energy of the open-pit office. The eager young business reporters were in constant motion, either talking rapid-fire on their headset phones or tapping out copy at one of the multiple monitors at each workstation. They paused only for bathroom breaks and snacks from the smorgasbord of salads, sandwiches, fruit, yogurt, and cold drinks that were laid out every day. Who had time for a sit-down lunch?

Until then, Baza's idea of workspace had come from the factory his family owned in Honduras. It had smokestacks, dirty metal floors, and that rank, all-pervading smell of old machine oil. The workers there always nodded and smiled when they saw him, but they had a beleaguered look that made him wonder how hard his father worked them.

Everyone toiling at Bloomberg had smooth hands and clean fingernails. The place reeked, but only of influence, reach, and power.

As the editor was escorting Baza and his father out to the elevator, Bloomberg himself hovered into view, wearing a wide smile. He peppered Baza senior with a few questions about investment in Central America and told Baza, "Come back and see us when you graduate, young man," as they shook hands good-bye.

The Bloomberg connection didn't come up again until Baza was about to get his MBA. While he was meeting with his NYU adviser about jobs on Wall Street, Baza ventured, "You know, I met Michael Bloomberg once and he actually suggested I apply for a job there when I finished school. But no one there would remember."

"Funny you should mention him," his counselor said. "I was just thinking that I should send you over to see my old friend Larry Wright, who is now the Mayor's Chief of Staff."

Something about Wright's air of purpose, layered over Baza's memory of Bloomberg's no-nonsense candor, was appealing. Baza also liked the idea of taking a detour from the expected path. Everyone assumed he would go to work on Wall Street, but he went to City Hall instead. His grandfather, the longtime Social Democrat from Honduras, would have been pleased, but his father, a modern capitalist, was more skeptical.

"Whenever politics is involved, it's trouble," Baza senior grumbled. "Is this why we sent you to America? To be a wage slave for some politician who will get kicked out next time around? If you want to operate under the dome of political corruption, you can do that right here in Honduras."

But Baza still had some of his youthful idealism. He saw affordable housing as a worthwhile use of his talents and education—more worthwhile, one might argue, than simply making money. A quick study, he soon learned the ins-and-outs of the Bloomberg style of affordable housing development. The Mayor followed in the tradition of Rudy Giuliani, relying on private investment as the engine for housing creation.

Baza also brought an element of financial creativity to his job. He became known as the one at City Hall who best understood how multiple public funding streams and private financing could be combined to the greatest advantage. "I swear, Ponce," exclaimed one of the major apartment developers he worked with, "on your calculator, one plus one equals three."

Within three years, Baza had not only been named Director of Affordable Housing, but had also gained some renown as a smart, disciplined manager who could size up a deal in minutes. He had a natural leadership style that blossomed in the rough-and-tumble negotiations surrounding big-time real estate deals. Attentive and astute, rather than loud and bombastic, Baza attracted genuine admiration from his colleagues as well as the big shots at City Hall. It didn't hurt that he was a young, hard-working immigrant with an obviously Hispanic name.

Baza also had an eye for uncovering scams and fraud in the system. Many private developers applied for city property tax credits for building low-cost housing, but then reneged or cut corners on agreements to make the units affordable. The young housing director had no fear of blowing the whistle, angering the worst offenders, but also building respect. He was on good terms with most of the movers and shakers who were rebuilding the Manhattan skyline, and amassed huge profits along the way.

Just before boarding the 6 train and heading uptown, Baza's immediate superior, Rita Ortez, the Mayor's Deputy and right arm, had asked to have a word with him in her office. He wasn't concerned in any way, there were often matters that Rita preferred to discuss with Baza behind closed doors. He took the usual worn leather upright chair to the right of her desk piled high with reports and papers. Rita preferred to work in an environment of controlled chaos. Whereas Baza couldn't think if his pens weren't lined up correctly and his desk surface wasn't clear of anything extraneous, Rita seemed to swim through stacks of papers, yet somehow always seemed to know the exact location of the thing she needed.

Baza noticed her expression was unusually terse. He smiled, hoping his ease would relax her a bit. He thought she was probably overworked and most likely hadn't even taken the full amount of vacation days she had accrued in her years of service with the Mayor.

"So, you wanted to chat, Rita?"

"Baza, I don't like these kinds of conversations so I'm not going to beat around the bush."

Baza suddenly felt a flush of heat under his suit jacket and glanced toward the window to see if it was open.

"IT has let me know there has been some unauthorized access to sites through company computers from your IP address. It's not immediately clear to me what these sites are but it appears it might have something to do with gambling."

Baza let out an involuntarily nervous chuckle, and shook his head, feeling immediately relieved. "I can assure you Rita, there must be some mistake, I am not a gambling man."

"Whatever it is Baza, this is your one and only warning, and I urge you to get some help. That's all I have to say on the matter. Other than that, keep up the good work. If you'll excuse me, I actually need to be on a conference call, like 10 minutes ago."

"Of course, Rita, no problem. Thank you," Baza scooted himself out of her office, took the stairs all the way down to the ground floor, and strode into the late afternoon sunshine, taking in gulps of the brisk air.

As he waited on the subway platform for the uptown train, he pondered the irony of the misdirected accusation that he might have a gambling problem. The exchange with Rita cemented a growing feeling that it was indeed time to move on from the Mayor's Office, before the ball started hitting closer to home. He had gotten all there was to get out of his experience there and was grateful for the opportunities he'd had with the Mayor.

But if there was one thing that could make a huge difference in his life and protect him, if a worst-case scenario situation was ever to arise, it would be him being able to be financially independent. Meaning, free from any money worries; able to help his family back in Honduras and fulfill his father's wishes and expectations for him, with enough money to allow Baza to live the life he wanted to live, without looking over his shoulder constantly and for fear someone was going to rip that rug out from under him. He had forgotten his father's wish that he help take the family's business into some new directions.

Baza was on his way to view a condo overlooking Central Park. His colleague, Joe, had put him onto the realtor he was about to meet. Baza was growing tired of his sorry-looking bachelor pad in the Village. It sounded like a good deal, although bargains were rare in the hot New York housing market. The building was only a short walk from the Plaza, the Pierre and the Ritz-Carlton.

The real estate broker, a fast-talking woman named Shelly Cohen, was waiting for him out front. She fit the mold perfectly. Looking to be in her early sixties, she had big hair, a grating New York accent, and a bottomless supply of patter about the state of the housing market. "There has *never* been a better time to buy," she insisted repeatedly. Many New York brokers talked as though they were economists or market experts of some sort, even if they'd spent most of their adult years as executive secretaries, housewives, or rock band promoters.

She hunted through a jangling ring of keys and found the one unlocking the unit, 5E. A one-bedroom on the fifth floor, it had no view, but was recently remodeled with a new bathroom, sleek-looking kitchen and double-paned windows. The whole building was Wi-Fi-equipped. On the list of amenities were an in-house dry cleaner and an ample staff of middle-aged white doormen, elevator operators, and front desk personnel, all ready and eager to meet his every need. But all that service and goodwill came at a price; Baza inwardly cringed when he saw that the co-op fee was $1,400 a month.

The broker was relentless in her boosterism. "Like my Uncle Norman always said, 'Buy property, they're not making any more of it,'" she blathered. Baza knew the quip had been lifted from Will Rogers. In fact, his property law professor at NYU had opened the semester's first class by scrawling the quote on the blackboard. He had followed with a serious lecture on the Dutch mania for speculating in tulip bulbs back in the 1600s, drawing parallels with the way New Yorkers were buying real estate.

As Baza would learn soon enough, the Manhattan real estate market was fueled by self-styled experts whose gassy pronouncements only helped to inflate the bubble. No one was looking over their shoulders to see if they were telling the truth. Most often, they were not.

Anxious to escape Cohen's oily grasp, Baza went through the motions of thanks as she stuffed a half-dozen business cards into his palm. The photo on the card had been doctored to show a woman at least 20 years younger than the real Shelly, who was now rushing to shut off the lights and close the blinds.

"If you like this unit, my advice is to make an offer well over asking, and do it right away. The market's not going to wait for you," said Cohen with a conspiratorial air and a big wink. "I've had tons of interest and it's going to be snapped up any minute now."

"What bullshit," thought Baza. Even this morning as he'd considered the listings Cohen had sent him, he wasn't sure whether deciding to put his own assets into the real estate market automatically allied him with the boosters. It wasn't long before he found himself arguing against the growing number of market detractors who insisted housing prices were dangerously over-inflated.

Baza wandered a few blocks east and turned south on Lexington Avenue, which he always preferred to Park or Fifth, where he felt outclassed. Lex Ave was like Honduras, whereas Park was more like Argentina and Fifth was like Brazil. He walked for a good 35 blocks as he peered into shop windows. He was on the lookout for a birthday gift for his younger sister, Veronica, who was turning 21 in two weeks. She was a student at Duke and would be thrilled, he knew, by a surprise gift in the mail.

It was just about cocktail hour when he reached the Gramercy Park Hotel, a *haute*-Bohemian haunt near Union Square. Inside was the Rose Bar, a dark little joint with plush red velvet drapes and a collection of art by the likes of Andy Warhol, Jean-Michel Basquiat, Keith Haring, Richard Prince, Damien Hirst, and Julian Schnabel.

Baza sidled up to the bar, half-relieved that it was nearly empty—it was still early. He sat alone with his tequila, which he never ordered when with his gringo friends; he wanted to avoid any chance of being mistaken for Latino trash. For the same reason, he always made a point of voicing his dislike for Mexican food.

As Baza tapped on his Blackberry, a stocky man with a ruddy complexion suggesting some Irish or Scottish lineage, strutted into the bar, sweat beading on his brow. His tie was loose and his pin-striped suit was rumpled. He noisily shuffled the empty stools, making room to position his broad body at the Terrazzo marbled-glass bar. He moved with stiff legs and his torso cocked forward from the hips—just like Big Bird from Sesame Street, Baza thought.

"What beers do you serve?" Big Bird asked the bartender. "Not Mexican, though."

The somewhat flamboyant bartender, sporting a well-coiffed handlebar mustache, rattled off a long list of beers the same way a first-grader recites the alphabet: Abita Amber, Ale Mary, Alley Cat, Amstel Light, Anchor Liberty, Anchor Steam, Becks, Heineken, O'Fallon's Gales and K Cider."

"An Alley Cat in one of those big mugs, like that one up there; a glass of ice water back," he said, pointing a stumpy finger toward a high shelf full of glasses.

He surveyed the bar, turning quickly from side to side. As his gaze settled on Baza, he asked, "Visiting New York? Staying in the hotel?"

"No, I live nearby," said Baza politely.

"Ah," said the man. "It looks like you're drinking Cuervo Gold, my favorite."

"Yes," said Baza, who was curious about the man, but also found the big man's presence disruptive. It broke into the mental grinding that occupied part of Baza's brain whenever he was alone. The committee in his head was always working overtime, worrying over the fears, concerns, and troubles that constantly afflicted him. The things he worried about almost never happened; yet his worries were his constant companions, never leaving his side for a minute.

His formula for relief was a few drinks and a conversation with a stranger in an upscale bar. One of his Honduran friends, Pedro Sandoval, who also migrated to the states for college, summed up American bar hopping this way: "Visit strange cities, hang out in strange bars, meet strange women and tell them lies about who you are and what your intentions may be." Baza would embellish only slightly, but for Pedro and other nighttime comrades, deceit came easy.

It seemed the Irishman was also looking for distraction. "I'm Mike Mayberry...good to meet you. What do you do here in New York?" he asked, extending a beefy hand.

"I work in the Mayor's office," said Baza, thinking to himself, *maybe not for much longer*. Though he still felt proud of his association with the Mayor. The king of Wall Street information services had become the most popular and, arguably, the most effective mayor New York City had ever had. "And who pays your bar bills?" he returned the question as he felt the glow of the tequila circulating through his compact frame.

"At Moody's, on the mortgage-backed securities desk, the hottest spot on Wall Street," Mayberry said, pushing out his broad chest against straining shirt buttons.

By now, the big man was slugging down his third beer and asking the harried bartender for the scotch menu. The barkeep, who had given Baza the once-over when he arrived, was now hustling to handle the swelling crowd, your typical Union Square demographic of good-looking, almost-wealthy, hip young adults who often text-messaged their mothers several times a day. The bartender seemed annoyed by Mayberry and gave Baza a disapproving look for associating with him. Mayberry kept turning and moving around as though he ought to be wearing a "wide load" sign.

"You should give up public service and get a real job," laughed Mayberry, giving Baza a manly wink and a light punch to the upper arm.

"Do you really think that a city bureaucrat has the stuff for shaping global finance?" replied Baza, flattered by his suggestion. He often used self-deprecation to disarm business associates. Many immigrants have too much pride to make fun of themselves, but Baza had quickly learned that Americans were taken by his humble charm.

"Actually, I believe you know my friend, Larry Wright," Mayberry said.

"Of course I do, you know him?" Baza was surprised to find any common connection.

"I just put two and two together and realized you must be the hotshot manager he's always going on about."

"Well, I don't know about that," Baza demurred, but inside felt his pride swell.

"Larry will kill me, but seriously, you should think about joining Moody's. The base salaries are good, the bonuses are fat, and we work and play around the clock. There's no better place to be right now. U.S. home mortgages are the best investment in the world, and Moody's makes it happen. We rate sixty percent of it," boasted Mayberry.

It was true that Moody's was the top credit rating agency, rating billions of dollars of bonds every day for companies big and small, as well as government agencies. The firm also rated the pools of securities created by financial institutions.

"Housing is our biggest growth area," Mayberry explained. "We're riding the wave of securitization and making a boatload of money doing it." Once banks and lending institutions had realized they could raise capital by packaging their mortgage holdings as bonds or securities that could be sold to investors, nearly all of them had jumped on the bandwagon. As the premier bond-rating organization, Moody's had a substantial piece of the action.

The trend was bound to take hold. Mortgage-backed bonds typically had a better yield than high-grade corporate bonds with similar terms, and their credit risk was low. Things really took off in 2003, when lenders began offering mortgages with ridiculous terms: zero down payment, short-term adjustable home loans that could change every month, or interest-only mortgages, or balloon-like loans that started out small for two years and then skyrocketed for the next 28.

Wall Street's financial engineering enabled lenders to sell the rights to receive the loan payments—that is, to "securitize" the mortgages they held. These mortgage-backed securities would then be rated by Moody's or one of the other two large rating agencies and sold to investors on Wall Street. It no longer mattered to lenders whether homebuyers would actually make their mortgage payments. Once the loans were packaged and sold, that became someone else's problem.

Baza felt a surge of interest but didn't want to appear too eager to know more just yet. Could this be the answer to his ambitions for financial independence from everything that could potentially bring him down? Could this drunk giant of a man hold a golden key to his future?

By the time Big Bird drained his fourth beer, he had decided that Baza belonged on his mortgage-backed securities desk. "Here, give me your number, and I'll text you mine," he insisted, punching his iPhone's touchscreen with pudgy fingers as he unsteadily got up to go. "Call me tomorrow and I'll set you up with HR."

Mayberry left Baza staring at the phone and wrestling with the conflicting emotions of desire and revulsion. A plum job on Wall Street was everything he had wanted, but at the same time, the idea of betraying his family's bent towards social justice causes was hard to swallow. He came from wealthy stock, but it was stock that held a deeply abiding social conscience. However, he felt fairly sure his father would be impressed with the gravitas and prestige that would come with a potential position at Moody's. Yet already he knew he wasn't going to pass up the chance to investigate the opportunity further.

It was muggy and overcast the day of Baza's interview at Moody's, which was housed in the reconstructed 7 World Trade Center in lower Manhattan. He took the 1 train from Union Square and stopped at his favorite food cart on 19th Street to grab a coffee.

As he reached in his pocket to pull out some money, several bills dropped to the ground. Baza bent to retrieve them, then jumped back with a start. A huge dun-colored rat with twitching whiskers darted out from beneath the cart, passing less than a foot from his hand. He recoiled in disgust.

Baza was surprised by his own reaction. He felt like he had jumped a little too high in the face of a simple rate. Surely, he had already lived in New York long enough to have had his share of rat sightings. Most of them usually occurred late at night, when passing by a mound of garbage bags on the sidewalk, waiting to be picked up the sanitation department, whenever they got around to it. Besides, Baza prided himself on having more refined manners than the average North American man. When out in public or in social settings, he was invariably calm and relaxed, despite the private bouts of anxiety that gripped him whenever he felt the urge to do something of which he knew his parents would disapprove.

His mother always said, "Mi Baza will find a good woman because he is a good man."

Baza was raised on a 55,000-acre ranch five miles north of the capital of Honduras, Tegucigalpa. He was the eldest of the four children, having two younger sisters and a brother. Honduras is a small country of only 43,000 square miles, about the size of the state of Nevada, with a population of 6.6 million. Life expectancy there is age 64 for men and 68 for women. Baza was not only increasing his families' financial prospects by taking New York by the horns, but perhaps increasing their genetic footprint, as well.

He had been well taken care of at home. Although decades of foreign investment in Honduras had steadily crowded out local business interests, undercutting the power and wealth of the country's upper class, Baza's family was still on top of their particular heap. They carried on the traditions of the old Honduran elite, who for the last century had been rural landholders in the highlands and valleys. Most of the wealthy families had gradually succumbed to the pull of urban life, but the Ponce family still preferred to live on its massive *hacienda*, which stretched from the country's western mountain range to the Caribbean Sea in the east.

The Ponce's, who had established their banana plantations in the early 1900s, had been one of the few Honduran family dynasties to ally with the foreign banana companies almost as soon as they arrived. The family's strongest ties were with the Chiquita Banana Company, which later became part of Procter and Gamble. That partnership was forged largely because Baza senior saw it as the only way to protect his family's business from new entrants with newer technology, more modern production systems, and better access to major markets. From him, Baza absorbed the notion that you had to keep your wits about you at all times if you didn't want to lose what you had.

The Ponce family was an attractive partner to foreign interests like Chiquita because of their long connection with indigenous workers, a critical labor pool. While wealthy Hondurans typically avoided the Caribbean lowlands, which were infamous for their oppressive heat and rural poverty, the Ponce's lived there in harmony with the native people. As long as Baza could remember, he had been taught to treat the indigenous Hondurans with dignity and respect. It was only right, the family felt, given the prosperity they reaped from the land.

The Ponce's were consequently not very good at joining hands with the other rich landowners, most of whom would use a heavy hand or a club when needed to get their way. Baza's family preferred to negotiate with and appease the workers and small rural land-owners. In the eyes of the elites, the Ponce clan was "simpatico" with the natives. Baza's father would say, "Our health and wealth depends on their mood, their happiness and their well-being."

Many of the elites were staunchly conservative, but the Ponce's were openly liberal, backing the kinds of economic development that would benefit Hondurans of all classes. The family even supported striking workers who confronted foreign-owned corporations and advocated social changes to ease the unrest. Baza's character was shaped by his parents' rejection of the excesses and sense of entitlement so evident in other wealthy families.

Still, the Ponce family did not pass up opportunities to broaden its economic reach and diversify its fortunes over the years. They began growing cotton and branched out into livestock when beef markets opened up after World War II. They made a second fortune from cattle production, an industry that tripled in Honduras from 1950 to 1980.

The family prospered in part by staying attuned to changes in the political climate. In the mid-1950s, the Honduran military was transformed, with the help of the United States, from a loose-knit, fragmented militia, to an organized national force. Baza's father kept close ties to military leaders, figuring the association would be a good one in the event of political unrest.

In the 1970s, the elder Baltazar joined progressive military, labor, and peasant groups who were supporting a reformist military regime. These coalitions kept social unrest to a minimum and the Ponce family fortune intact.

"Peace is the best thing that could ever happen to this family," Baza's father would insist. "If trouble starts, always remember that the less attention, drama and disgrace you bring to this family, the better."

Baza paid for the coffee, tried to put the rat out of his mind, and kicked himself for giving the idea of bad omens any kind of credence. He told himself he just hated rats, pure and simple. He had once read that the Romans considered white rats a good omen and black or brown rats a bad omen. Other than in a pet store, he had never seen a white rat in New York, but he'd noticed that the bad-omen type was becoming increasingly visible. They also seemed to be getting bigger and bolder, as if they, too, wanted to go after a larger piece of the prosperity pie.

He wondered whether the rat population was actually growing or whether he'd simply become more aware of their presence. Reviews of a new book, straightforwardly titled "Rats," had been drawing attention to the rodent phenomenon.

For decades, Moody's had operated from a modest space on Church Street, one block south of Ground Zero. "Credit: Man's Confidence in Man" was emblazoned on a bronze plaque that had been installed at the entrance of the stubby old building upon its completion in 1951. The words were a quote from John Moody, founder of the firm. Below that was a quotation from U.S. Senator Daniel Webster: "Credit is the vital air of the system of modern commerce. It has done more – a thousand times more – to enrich nations than all of the mines of the world."

The messages were clear: credit is good, and credit is about trust.

It was not until his studies at Dartmouth that Baza fully understood the uses of debt and financial leverage. His family adhered to a strict rule of owning all assets outright, and they would not have dreamed of intentionally risking any of their holdings in an effort to compound their wealth.

Of course, the family did engage in short-term borrowing when necessary, and Baza's father certainly understood the concept of debt. But the family was more motivated to preserve its capital than to grow it by taking risks, even calculated ones.

While studying at NYU, Baza had read George Soros's book, *The Alchemy of Finance,* and eagerly attended an on-campus lecture by the legendary investor. Soros pounded the drum about the Bush Administration and its many missteps after 9/11, but he also discussed leverage and economic bubbles, imparting principles Baza did not forget.

"As prices rise, the same collateral can support a greater amount of credit," Soros had said. It made sense. If you put 10 percent down on a $100,00 house and its value went up to $200,000, you could borrow another $100,000 with no additional equity at stake. That was leverage at its best, and also at its worst.

The word leverage comes from the French word "lever," meaning "to lift." Just as a lever is used to increase the mechanical force applied to a physical object, financial leverage uses debt to increase the power of the equity applied to purchase, thereby creating more value. The trick is to make sure that the added return exceeds the cost of the debt.

Leverage was a modern innovation: instead of paying as you go, you borrow to have more as you go.

In spite of his ingrained mistrust of debt and risk, Baza's father had encouraged his son to study modern economics in the U.S., the goal being in part to help advance the family fortunes. It was understood that this would entail learning how principles of leverage might best be applied to those fortunes.

The senior Baza was continually worried about threats to the Ponce dynasty from Honduras's internal political strife, hostile neighbors, and vulnerability to the machinations of multinational corporations. This made him doubly unsure about how to go about expanding the family's business interests. Bankers kept proposing novel ways to build the family's wealth, but he did not trust or understand what they were selling, and so he didn't act on any of the recommendations.

As Baza's business and financial knowledge grew, he sent his father a raft of ideas, and they spent countless hours discussing them. But there was never a major deal or project that they could agree upon.

They watched with interest as a family-owned furniture company in North Carolina threw a significant chunk of its assets into a venture-backed Internet start-up in 2001—and then with alarm, as the family lost it all in the dot-com bust. Stories such as that one gave both of them pause. They had also read how the Chandler Family, owners of the *Los Angeles Times,* created a venture fund to invest in technologies of the future. But the jury was still out on its performance.

After a few years in New York, Baza had learned much about managing leverage, debt, and risk. But he had concluded that Honduras was a different world from New York, and it was courting trouble to mix the two. The closest the family had gotten to foreign investments was buying New York real estate—two apartment buildings in Manhattan, Baza's townhouse downtown, which he thought he would rent out to students or artists if he moved uptown, and a second home in the Hamptons. But that was as far out on the limb as they had gone.

Baza stopped briefly to straighten his tie before checking in with Moody's receptionist.

"ID, please," said the security guard in a flat voice. Baza pulled out his driver's license, trying hard not to feel nervous. Even though he entered the U.S. as a privileged Ivy League student, being an immigrant always made him feel somehow vulnerable.

"Who are you visiting?"

"Elizabeth Cardenas in HR."

After dialing the number twice, the guard said, "Voicemail; they'll call down." He went back to discussing the Mets with his fellow guard.

Baza stood at the desk and crossed his arms, annoyed at the way he'd been dismissed.

He watched as Moody's employees—the drones, the go-getters, and the ones nursing hangovers—filed into the building. He began to count smiles. It was his technique for distracting himself during moments of boredom. His surveys showed surprising variance in smile ratios, depending on the city, the time of day, and, of course, the weather. In this crowd, six out of 50 were smiling. Not a bad ratio, but then, it was still early.

Just then, Michael Mayberry strutted in with a smile stretched across his beefy face. He carried an expensive-looking but banged-up briefcase. Baza was happy to see the effusive big man just before his interview. It made him feel like it was a good sign. They had met up briefly the previous night so Mayberry could prep him for the interview today. During the course of the evening, Baza had internally nicknamed him Big Bird, from the children's TV show of the 1970s, due to his gangling presence.

"Well, well, if it isn't my new South American comrade."

"Central American," Baza smiled.

"Right—Honduras. I remember. It's wedged in there somewhere between Mexico and Brazil," said Big Bird in a loud whisper as he leaned in Baza's direction, "just like I was wedged in between these two crazy Russian girls last night. They drank my booze, ate my ice cream, and took one of my down pillows. Can you believe it, stealing someone's pillow? Don't they have geese back in Putinland?"

Big Bird lived with his wife, three children, and two dogs in a five-bedroom Colonial in Greenwich, Connecticut. He also kept a pied-à-terre on Madison Avenue between 31st and 32nd. Frequented by drug dealers and hookers before Giuliani became mayor, the neighborhood was now dotted with boutique hotels and expensive condos.

The security guards chuckled. Big Bird gave the guard a nod, grabbed Baza's arm and ushered him through the security checkpoint.

"Your meeting will be in HR on floor forty-two; I'm in the executive suites up on sixty-four. Come up and see me before you leave and I'll show you around. And remember, be chirpy. They say they like serious people around here, but they really don't."

Unsure that he had the capacity to be "chirpy," Baza smiled and waved weakly to Big Bird. He despised having favors handed to him by an operator like Mayberry, just as he hated the elevator system in Moody's high-rise quarters. You punched in your destination in the lobby, and the system directed you to a particular elevator bank. When your elevator arrived and the sign above it lit up, you simply entered and waited for it to take you to your floor. There was no way to press the key for your floor because there was no need to do so; the elevator was pre-programmed to take you where you were going. This system was undeniably more efficient, but took a central element of control away from the user.

In many ways, the workings of the elevator system resembled the risk/return models that credit analysts like Moody's used to rate securities, Baza mused. Like the pre-programmed elevator, the models simply gave you a result. You had no control—not even a real understanding of why the numbers came out the way they did. The idea was that, with the right inputs and programming, the models were more objective and efficient than human judgment could ever possibly be.

Thanks to his work in the Mayor's Office of Housing and Redevelopment, Baza was already well-versed in financial modeling, He'd punch in some assumptions about the likelihood that a given set of landlords would repay their debts to the city. Out popped the terms of the muni bonds. Much like Moody's elevators, the risk levels were pre-programmed, taking bond investors to the floor of the return they wanted. It was simple in one sense, but complex if you actually wanted to think it all through.

Baza was greeted on the 42nd floor by Cardenas's assistant, Leni Hauptmann, a tall, attractive blonde with a German accent. She also had a sexy gap between her two front teeth, a crooked smile, and one eye that wandered slightly. Somehow, these defects only enhanced her appeal to Baza. He felt a familiar stirring in his pants, prompting him to seek the restroom before his meeting.

"Through that door, then take the first right, just across from the conference room. I will meet you back here," Leni said.

Baza recalled Big Bird's description of Leni from the interview prep session. A transplant from Berlin, Leni had cosmopolitan attitudes toward sex and an active erotic imagination that was triggered the instant she met an interesting man. When she'd had a few drinks, she liked to regale co-workers with her lusty and explicit fantasies featuring other colleagues.

Big Bird would often be part of a Moody's gang going out for drinks after work, and he was an especially enthusiastic audience for Leni's tales, always prodding her for more.

"*Ja,* if it were you, I would walk you to church, take you to confession and leave you with the priest," she would reply with a smirk. "Bad Irish boys like you don't get to have fun...only penance, nothing more."

"But then you should take me home and spank me, don't you think?" pleaded Big Bird, hoping to incite some more randy conversation.

"No! No spanking! Just you and the priest in the confessional, that's it," Leni would say soberly.

Standing at the urinal, Baza finished too quickly and dripped a spot the size of a ping-pong ball on his light brown pants. He rubbed the spot with a paper towel, which left shredded remnants on the fabric, only making things worse. He could do nothing but button his jacket and dangle his hands awkwardly in a lame attempt to cover up.

"Are you ready? Would you like coffee, tea, or bottled water?" asked Leni. She touched his arm, signaling him to walk in front of her as they moved down the hall to Ms. Cardenas's office.

"Welcome, Mr. Ponce, please have a seat, have you been offered something to drink?" said Cardenas with the air of someone who had gone through the same routine several hundred times before. She was a 40-something statuesque woman with the brusque manner of an accomplished middle manager. "So, Mayberry sent you... that's great. He seems to think you're a good fit for Moody's. How do you two know each other?" she continued at top speed, seeming not interested at all in the specifics of Baza's acquaintance with Big Bird. She struck Baza as someone who preferred to hear herself talk.

Cardenas spent twenty minutes describing Moody's and the position Baza was being considered for, then handed him a written job listing. "Chief Analyst: Mortgage-Backed Securities Rating Desk. Requirements: MBA plus five to seven years of direct experience in housing-related securities in a financial capacity and with progressively greater responsibilities."

She then listened for perhaps two minutes as Baza summed up his résumé, cutting him off with a clipped comment.

"Impressive background... Say, by the way, do you happen to know Roberta McDougall? She also graduated from Dartmouth in ninety-eight, though she studied art history and never mentioned hanging around with any of you biz guys."

Baza's mind flashed back to his years at Dartmouth and he was struck by the thought that he didn't even recall any of the women he met on campus during his time there.

"Anyway...What are your two, three and five-year goals, and why do you want to work for Moody's?" She reverted to the standard HR playbook.

"I'm interested in exploring creative financial models and I'd love to grow with a firm as venerable as Moody's," he said, hoping he was striking the right notes of interest and thoughtful modes of discourse.

"Very good. Those are the kinds of qualities we look for in a role such as this." She looked at him briefly without betraying any emotion. She seemed perfectly cast in the mold of a female corporate bureaucrat. He looked for sweat stains under the arms of her silk blouse, but saw no sign of them.

"Thank you, Mr. Ponce," she said, as she stood up and pushed back her chair, signaling an end to the interview. "You seem to be a strong candidate for the job and I'd like you to meet with some others in the department."

Always one to do his homework, Baza had made sure to research the history of the firm before putting in his application.

The son of an ice salesman, John Moody was a financial journalist who had an epiphany. In 1900, he began publishing background information on a variety of stocks and bonds. His publication became popular but went under when the stock market fell in 1907.

He decided to give the business another go and began analyzing the creditworthiness of railroad companies.

For years, the business grew based on profits from subscriptions to Moody's publications. But by the 1970s, the financial markets had become so complex that the firm had to expand the ranks of its analysts greatly.

Unable to cover its staffing needs with subscription revenues, Moody's switched to a new business model: It began charging bond issuers a fee to rate their securities. That set up a conflict of interest that would come back to haunt the company 35 years later. It was a classic case of letting the fox into the henhouse—or at the very least, making it easier for the fox to get in whenever he wanted.

But in the interim, Moody's reaped the rewards from a thriving, high-growth business. The rating process became increasingly efficient, thanks to complex computer models that gauged the risk of each issuance and summed up its creditworthiness according to a system of letter ratings. Ratings went from Triple-A, for the highest-quality investment-grade paper, down to C or D for what came to be known as "junk bonds."

At the same time, the firm's market expanded dramatically as trading volumes rose and new types of bonds were devised, most notably, the mortgage-backed security.

It was a Salomon Brothers trader named Lewis Ranieri who created the first mortgage-backed securities in the late 1980s. Ranieri, who was also known for the prodigious quantities of cheeseburgers he was able to consume, figured out how to take a diverse mix of home loans, representing different borrowers in different locations with different loans at varying rates, and bundle them into a standardized bond.

Investors were slow to warm to the concept, but once they did, they fell all over each other for the chance to put assets into this marvelous new investment vehicle. It offered great returns and the promise of security—never mind that the assurances were about as credible as your local real estate agent becoming a quantum physicist.

As the *Financial Times* of London explained Ranieri's genius in one of its articles, "He knew the magic of structuring was in the packaging. If packaged in the right way, mortgages created a huge, new tradable bond market."

In order to be sold, these bonds needed to be rated—and that's where Moody's came in. It was the largest and most respected rating agency—a rock-solid institution deemed to be as dependable as death and taxes. Rating-mortgage backed securities and other types of collateralized debt obligations, or CDOs, became a big business for Moody's, driving its growth for more than two decades.

Mortgage-backed securities were the darlings of the debt market, partly because they held something for everyone. They enabled lenders to collect substantial loan fees while offloading all risks of default. Investors loved the idea that bundling diverse mortgages made risk levels dwindle. And for the ratings agencies including—and especially—Moody's, they were tantamount to a money machine.

Baza was impressed with Moody's operation, and all four of the executives he met with seemed to be impressed with him, particularly his accomplishments at City Hall. Three of the four asked whether he had met the Mayor, which he had on many occasions, and then offered up anecdotes of their own encounters with Michael Bloomberg.

But he spent the most time with his prospective boss, Dana Fielding, a tall, angular woman who seemed genuinely eager to connect with him. She slumped as she talked, probably as a result of too many years of being called "beanpole" in school.

Baza hoped his experience in the Mayor's office impressed Fielding, but she seemed more taken with his interest in mathematics. His résumé listed the Dartmouth Math Club among his activities.

"Still involved with Dartmouth?"

"I occasionally attend alum functions and go for a drink at the Dartmouth Club over on Vanderbilt," he replied.

"Fantastic, I am very involved with the Penn Club, it's just around the corner. If you come on board, I'll take you to lunch at the grill there."

After an hour with Fielding, Baza decided he would enjoy working on her team. She clearly loved her work, strived for excellence in everything she did, and seemed to care about the people who worked for her genuinely.

After leaving Fielding, Baza rode an elevator to the 64th floor. He was told Mayberry was in a meeting and could not be disturbed. But just as he was leaving, he heard a loud voice behind him.

"Hey, Mr. Big Shot! I hear you wowed the folks at the ratings desk. I think you're gonna get a really nice offer. You owe me, dude," Big Bird said as he strode up and clasped Baza's hand. "Gotta run; I'm about to close the deal of my life with Merrill Lynch. I may get that tropical island yet."

2

While New York fulfilled Baza's desires for challenge and creativity, it also met other needs. A couple of days after the interview, even though he hadn't officially received an offer from Moody's yet, he was feeling positive about how the interview had gone and decided to indulge himself and kick back on the Lower Eastside with some of his drinking buddies from the Mayor's Office.

They chose a restaurant near First Avenue known for its lively bar scene. While waiting for his friends to show, Baza had already had a couple of Scotches. By the time everyone was sufficiently fortified with liquor and bar food, dinner was an afterthought. Saying goodnight, Baza headed off to Lucky Cheng's, where Felix the bartender would be holding court, cocktail shaker in hand.

"There he is, the Latino Donald Trump," Felix greeted him familiarly. "*Que pasa,* my friend?"

"Not much," said Baza woozily, feeling played out and drained of conversation. Without a word, Felix poured a Courvoisier V.S.O.P. and set it in front of him. Suddenly Baza's attention was roused, as a heavily made-up, 30-ish woman wearing a tight sheath dress and an armload of gold bracelets slid onto a bar stool, pulling up her skirt as she crossed her legs to show firm thighs. Before Baza could finish formulating his conversational gambit, a distinguished-looking older man took the spot next to her and greeted her with a kiss on the lips.

The Honduran downed his remaining cognac in one gulp and headed for the door. Revived by the brisk early spring air, he began to walk back toward Houston Street where he planned to get a cab. Yet he was not quite ready to go home to the solitude of his apartment, but also not quite sure what he was looking for. As he felt the low rumblings of a hunger for trouble, he drifted over towards the Bowery. Walking felt good. The neighborhood was peopled at this hour with some of the druggies, hookers and malcontents who shared the decaying neighborhood with struggling Asian and Latino immigrants and assorted casualties from the post-hippie era.

As he rounded the corner of Houston onto Chrystie Street, he spotted a gaggle of street girls of various ages and costumes in front of a raucous bar on the next block. As he drew closer, he realized this had to be Mama's, a prime hot spot for what gay activists called "the transgender community." Baza had heard of the place, but had never summoned the nerve to go there.

He drew closer to get a better look at the girls. Some were willowy and tall, easily topping six-feet-two; others were short and plump or beefy. He could tell they were transsexuals by the care they took in dressing to the nines. These girls were wearing more make-up, hotter clothes, and a trendier assortment of bling than any TS women that he'd ever seen this side of Las Vegas.

As Baza walked past the crowd, he felt a surge of interest and alarm. "Look at him, he's adorable! Come on over here, sugar!" said one, her bangle bracelets jangling as she threw him a come-hither gesture.

In his well-cut blazer and Italian shoes, Baza stood out among the Bowery crowd. He was torn between a desire to succumb and the impulse to flee. He kept walking for a few yards, but then hesitated for a second and glanced back toward the girls over his shoulder. That was all the invitation the tall girl in blue sequins needed. She minced over in her strappy silver high heels and grabbed his arm, pulling him toward the door. "Come on inside where it's warmer, honey," she insisted. "We'll take care of you."

Mama's turned out to be a three-story den of temptation. The street level was a low-life dive bar. The second story was a more upscale and intimate dance floor where the Trans girls would dance together, taunting the men at the small bar in the rear. The top floor was full of beat-up couches where old drag queens would linger for hours, repairing their make-up and telling outrageous stories.

This was TS heaven, a hallucinatory mix of illusion and reality. Though femininity was the theme, only men or males in ladies' attire could be found there. The other patrons were mostly a bunch of perverted old men who leered at the transsexuals, trotting out hoary jokes while they tossed back shots and beers. Baza couldn't decide if he was repelled or fascinated.

Then he saw Trina—a diamond in the rough, he could tell from the first glance. She was five-feet-eight with a compact, muscular body and an elegant way of putting her cheap, glitzy clothes together. Her copper-colored polyester-satin halter dress set off her smooth, well-buffed arms and shoulders. You could tell she was from Hawaii by her island features and the *cafe-au-lait* sheen of her skin. Then there were her legs. They were long, perfectly feminine, and encased in sheer black nylons, just the way Baza liked them. He felt his body heat rising.

There was something else about her that he found hard to identify but to which he felt irresistibly drawn, some mixture of ineffable sadness and vulnerability combined with intelligence and fierce determination. In that instant, he wasn't fully aware of being able to read all this in her face. Yet it was a moment he would often look back to and how he would later describe Trina.

He ordered two vodkas, watching as the bartender poured the drinks from a screw-top bottle into heavy tumblers, and took them over to where Trina stood chatting amiably with some other girls. "You look to me like a woman who could use a little refreshment," he ventured, smiling in a way he hoped seemed sincere. "Honey, you have no idea!" she replied with a wink. Then, noting Baza's mannerly ways, she met his gaze and looked straight into his eyes. "Shall we go sit someplace quiet and talk?"

Bypassing the dance floor, Trina led Baza up another flight of stairs and to an unoccupied couch in the corner. They made a few minutes of small talk over the thrumming music, laughing about the bar, the crowd, and what it was like to be part of the TS scene in New York. As they talked, Baza eyed her long legs, held together delicately at the ankles and knees.

Suddenly Trina turned to him with a serious expression. Looking straight into his face, she said, "Can I ask you a question? You seem like a nice guy...and I can't help wondering what it is that's making you sad."

Baza was startled. This wasn't the kind of conversation he was accustomed to having with any of the women, TS or cis, he usually dated. But he could feel his inhibitions sliding away before Trina's attentive, open gaze, and alcohol always loosened his tongue. Haltingly at first, Baza told her of his childhood in Honduras, the expectations attached to his life of privilege, and his struggle against his unconventional urges.

Trina listened quietly, then took his hand. "Yes, I know what it's like to realize you'll never fit in," she said softly, then sat up with an abrupt motion. "...And now I've got to go," she said. The crowd was thinning out, and Baza realized it was far past midnight.

"At least give me your phone number," he stammered, feeling jerked away from her tenderness. Pulling a tiny golden pencil and a scrap of paper from her purse, Trina scrawled the number and started down the steps. "Don't worry," she said, "I know guys like you never call women like me."

Baza stammered. "No, I will." He suddenly didn't want himself to be lumped in with any of the other clients she might have or guys she dated. At the same time, he realized he must have sounded just like them. He thought it probably best if he said no more and let his actions speak louder than his words.

Three days after his interviews, Baza received an email from Cardenas with an attached PDF signed by Dana Fielding. "We are pleased to offer you the position of Director of Credit Analysis,

Mortgage-Backed Securities Division, Structure Finance Unit at Moody's. If you choose to accept this position you will be joining a world-class company that is reshaping financial markets around the globe."

Baza smiled as he read it. He swiveled in his chair, stretched, put his hands behind his neck and re-read the email, luxuriating in the glow of recognition and opportunity.

This was why he had come to the US. A better position, higher pay, the feeling that you could help make big things happen—these things, which seemed so unattainable in his home country, were at the heart of the American Way. It was all about blazing your own path to success by expecting more and working hard to get it.

This aspirational ethic seemed to him uniquely American. It was not widely exported. On the contrary, it was the magnet that drew thousands of legal and illegal immigrants to the U.S. each year, even at the price of immense struggle and hardship. America's appeal grew not from its freeways, malls, or reality TV, and not even from its mountains, forests, or beaches, but from its atmosphere of ambition.

He thought gratefully of Big Bird and how their chance meeting and the Irishman's compulsive gregariousness had led to this moment. Some of Big Bird's behaviors made him uncomfortable, it was true, but Baza figured their paths would not cross too much at work due to the natural conflict between sales and analytics. He would be happy to keep their friendship to the occasional lunch or round of drinks now and then.

As Fielding had explained the job being offered, he would be the Super-Analyst of Mortgage-Backed Securities, with two deputies and 75 junior analysts working under him. As he would learn, on the rare occasion when his group rated a security as a poor credit risk, his job title would be morphed into "Super Asshole."

The terms of Moody's offer were impressive when stacked against his City job, which gave him more clout than comp. On top of a base annual salary of $200,000, there was a 50 percent bonus if certain MBOs—targets set through "management by objectives"—were met. That meant "work hard, don't make any big mistakes, and if the company does well, so will you."

Baza's impulse was to hit "reply" and accept the offer immediately, but that kind of eagerness was not his style. He sat back, smiled, and let his mind linger over imagined scenes from his brilliant career on Wall Street. He wanted to call his mother with the news, but decided to wait a day. He wanted to hear the gush of pride in her voice through the phone, but he steeled himself to wait longer, fearing he might jinx it otherwise.

Submerged in his daydreams, he jumped when his cell phone played a ring tone from "Strangers in the Night." That meant an unknown caller.

"Hi Baza, this is Dana Fielding."

Startled, Baza sat up in his chair immediately. It was as if she had been standing over his shoulder, watching him open the email.

"I just wanted to congratulate you on the offer and encourage you to accept it, because I believe you can have an extremely rewarding career at Moody's. We are very excited about your joining us."

"Wow," Baza thought. "That could have been a recording." He wondered if she had written it down.

"Thank you very much, Dana, I was just sitting here trying to absorb it all. I really am very flattered by the opportunity," Baza said politely. "I just want to take a couple of days to sort out my options and make sure this is the right move for me. I hope you understand," he added.

The words that rolled from his mouth were so simple, so honest, that it gave Baza goosebumps, as he savored the success he was feeling. There was an awkward pause in the conversation.

"Great, take your time and we'll talk—let's say, by Friday. If in the interim you have any questions or there's anything you need, please don't hesitate to call. Take care...good-bye."

"Thank you, I will do that." Baza hung up.

Baza had also interviewed with Todd Bridges, EVP of the group. He had been at Harvard for both his undergrad degree and his MBA. On his wall were several Harvard plaques and his Harvard pendant, along with pictures of twin daughters and an infant son. "The perfect little life," thought Baza, without bitterness. That was not something he aspired to. His own personal life was under wraps and not for public display.

Given Bridges' lofty credentials, the interview was surprisingly lackluster, even inept. The EVP stumbled as he attempted a couple of lame questions about Honduras. He even asked Baza whether border crossings were challenging for him after 9/11. Baza answered, "no," and the interview ended soon after. At the time, it did make him wonder. If this is what the trajectory at Moody's led to, would joining the firm be a mistake? He had pushed the thought aside quickly, and it did not resurface when he received the offer.

But as Baza re-read the offer letter yet again, his initial euphoria was punctured by one sentence that set off alarm bells.

"This offer is subject to personal credit and criminal background checks. Please contact Penny House at Ext. 120, internal security, to complete the necessary financial and medical disclosures."

Baza's heart pounded, his cheeks flushed, and his mind began to race. "Oh God," he thought about his past visits to TS bars; credit card charges at infamous clubs, tests for sexually transmitted diseases, treatments for herpes. He could already anticipate the wording of the next email—the one that would rescind the job offer and place his name on the firm's blacklist for all time.

Despite the fact that Baza thought he'd never have anything to do with the executive from the 65th floor, it wasn't long before Mayberry and Baza became friends—more than that, a team. Together, they were like Batman and Robin; Mr. Inside and Mr. Outside; Good Cop and Bad Cop; Jack and Bobby; Bill Gates and Steve Balmer. There were also times when they more closely resembled Laurel and Hardy or Don Quixote and Sancho Panza.

During their first celebratory lunch after Baza was hired, He revealed that he had coined a nickname for Mayberry—Big Bird—which Mayberry accepted with a knee-slapping laugh.

Big Bird and Baza approached life from completely different directions. The hard-charging Irishman's world was all about aspiration; he was in the habit of reaching, climbing, and even clawing for what he wanted. Baza, on the other hand, was out to preserve what he had. He was most intent on protecting his class, wealth and standing against outside threats. As a result, he was constantly worried about being misinterpreted, about getting caught at something he had or had not done, or about someone else taking what he had. One was driven by ambition, the other by fear.

Yet despite their differences, they found things to like in each other. Baza could see that, beneath all the bluster, Big Bird was a canny businessman who never stopped thinking. Big Bird, for his part, admired Baza's keen mathematical mind as much as he envied his genteel ways.

Big Bird raised his glass and toasted him. "Stick with me," Mayberry said. "I'm going to enjoy having a smart fella like you around the place. You can teach me which fork to use. And we're going to make a lot of money together."

Even though Big Bird quickly learned that his new protégé came from wealth and privilege, he saw Baza's modesty as a shining contrast to the arrogance, ego, and aggressiveness of the Wall Street types who felt entitled to the obscene wealth they amassed. Mayberry still felt his working-class roots, and as much he strived for riches, he could not stomach the excesses and haughty attitudes of those around him.

In Manhattan, people with serious money could forget that the poor existed. Employment in the borough had become increasingly white collar, and as lower-end jobs were pushed out to Brooklyn, Queens, or Jersey, and the real estate market followed suit. The seediness of Times Square had been swept away in a tide of remodeling and construction; now the entire city was becoming safe and prosperous. One-bedroom condos in the restored Plaza Hotel on Fifth were quickly snapped up at $25 million a pop. Meanwhile, computer engineers from Bangladesh were buying $750,000 studios on the Upper Westside. The city had no bounds.

Neither Big Bird nor Baza had forgotten that poor people existed. Baza could easily picture himself back on the banana plantation among his father's Honduran workers, just as the low-paid clerks and bargain-shopping customers at his family store, Mayberry's, were still vivid in Big Bird's mind. This may have been part of what made them *simpatico*.

Baza found that there was one more way that he and Big Bird could relate. It turned out that, like Baza, the big Irishman found it difficult to tamp down his sexual urges. It only took two or three beers for Big Bird's sense of propriety to fall by the wayside as he leaned close to Baza and whispered, "I want to tell you how I learned to masturbate."

Baza recoiled slightly, wondering where this unexpected turn in the conversation would lead. Big Bird continued, undeterred.

"My brother taught me quite by accident.

"We shared a small room with bunk beds. I slept on the top, he slept on the bottom. One summer night when I was eleven, I was awakened in the middle of the night. The whole bed was shaking. There were no earthquakes where we lived, so I couldn't imagine what might cause the bed to rock so violently. It happened again the next night, and again the night after that.

"The following night, I decided I would get to the bottom of it. I took a flashlight to bed and when the bunks began to shake, I climbed down and shined a flashlight into the bed. There was my brother Jeff, and his face was bright red, all puffy and sweaty.

"What are you doing?" I demanded.

"He said, 'I've discovered something amazing. I may be the only person in the world who knows about this, except maybe some boy in Africa or someplace like that."

"'What is it?' I pressed him.

"'The Burst of Feeling,' he said."

Baza laughed out loud, as Big Bird looked at him knowingly. Baza's last shred of reserve drained away; he had found a friend.

"Oh, you mean people down there in Honduras masturbate, too?" Big Bird said. "I'm happy to hear it. At Moody's we don't hire anybody who doesn't."

Big Bird had already put in the call alerting William, his driver, to pull his massive black Cadillac Escalade up to the curb. He imagined that strangers on the street would think the vehicle was transporting a Russian Mafia boss, an ambassador, or a media tycoon. The car fit the fantasy, although Big Bird himself did not.

"This one's on me," he said over his shoulder as he walked toward the exit. "I'm off to break the bank with dinner at Rue 57—catch you soon."

Baza gleaned that Big Bird was trying to sound impressive and extravagant with the mention of Rue 57, but by chance, he had been to the establishment and knew it to be a modest café at 57th and Sixth, near the London Hotel, where his father often stayed on visits to New York. The restaurant was nice enough, with good breakfasts and outdoor tables in pleasant weather, but it was hardly the upscale eatery Big Bird had made it out to be.

It was a trivial deception—one so inconsequential, it was hardly worth noticing, Baza thought. But as time went on, he would have more than one occasion to remember it.

While Baza lived in a world of fears that were much of his own making, he came from a world that was anything but. Born into wealth and privilege, he was raised in a largely idyllic setting. The Ponce household became a gathering spot for generals, radical leaders and other progressive types, who would sit for hours, eating with the family and drinking Pisco Sours on the back veranda. Baza's father would occasionally organize hunting parties, leading groups of visitors in pursuit of ducks or wild boar. For most of his young life, Baza looked up to these men for their strength and *machismo*, especially the military leaders with their rows of medals and decorations.

The only deviant experience he could identify from his childhood took place when he was about 12, when his image of manhood was shaken to the core during one hunting expedition.

It was late in the day and Baza, tired from clambering through the hills, drifted away from the hunting party. Wandering solo on a ridge with a rifle in hand, he rounded a berm and came upon a scene his eyes could scarcely believe. There was General Manuel Martinez, the highest-ranking officer in the group, sprawled in the vetiver grass with Pedro, one of the Ponce family's young ranch hands. The two were lying clutched in a fevered embrace with their mouths pressed together and their pants down around their knees.

Baza knew Pedro as the effeminate 19-year-old son of Filipe Diago, who oversaw the Ponce family stables.

Baza stared for a moment, rubbing his eyes and trying to focus in the glare of the late afternoon light. Then, hit by the full impact of what he had witnessed, he wheeled around to run down the ridge toward the rest of the hunting party. Martinez yelled out to Baza as he hurriedly buttoned up his pants, pushing aside the hapless Pedro, who took off like a jackrabbit and didn't look back.

"Baza! Come here, my boy," called Martinez in a commanding, but quavering, voice. Baza stopped short and turned around, but did not move or look at the man's face. The General walked quickly toward him, averting his eyes as he scrambled to button up his shirt and jacket. Frozen in embarrassment and fear, Baza stood with his shoulders slumped, staring at the ground.

"Now we have a little secret, my friend Baza," said the General, still flushed with excitement. "You must keep to yourself what you saw here today, just the same as if it was a military secret. Can I count on you to be a patriot and not reveal this to anyone? Not your padre or mama...not a soul. Do you understand? I am counting on you to be a good soldier."

Baza blinked, stammered a few words, and ran off. He knew the General wanted only to save his own skin, but Baza would have said anything just to escape. His breath came in short gasps, and he felt a wave of nausea over his uncomfortable bargain with authority. It wasn't the last time Baza would make a deal that left him feeling compromised and unsure.

But if Baza's father had taught him anything, it was the overriding value of pragmatism. While Baza had been raised with a strong ethical code underscored by the priests and his teachers at school, he had also seen how compromises were sometimes necessary to serve a larger purpose. Intuitively, he knew that betraying the General's secret could undermine his family's ability to influence the larger scheme of things. The Ponce's had long seen it as their obligation—more than that, as their destiny—to help Honduras along a path of modernization that was not plagued by the excesses and unrest that plagued its neighbors to the north and south.

A few years after the incident with the General, in December of the year he turned 15, Baza's family traveled to New York for their annual shopping trip. It was part of their holiday tradition. Every year, the Ponce's would spend a week amid glittering boutiques and department stores, alternating between Paris, Rio, and Manhattan.

As Baza grew older, he was increasingly bored by shopping and sought every possible chance to go off and explore on his own. The day his mother planned to shepherd the family through Macy's famous flagship store at Herald Square, Baza was prepared.

Pointing out that he had already seen Macy's Christmas decorations twice before, he mentioned the Museum of Natural History, showed his wad of cab money, and swore to be back at the Plaza in time to change for dinner. His mother, ever protective, hesitated for a few seconds. Then she looked up at him with a nervous and slightly sheepish laugh.

"Oh, Bazito...it's true that you are almost a man, even though I still think of you as *mi hijo*," she said, her eyes softening. "You have a good head on your shoulders, I know. Just be careful...and leave a message at the hotel when you have lunch. Do it for me. All right, *querrido*?"

Baza murmured hasty agreement, slipped on his vicuna coat and muffler and hurried out the main hotel entrance. The air was clear and bracingly cold; each breath sent out a cloud of vapor. Jamming his hands in his pockets, he set off down Fifth Avenue in the opposite direction from the Natural History Museum, jubilant in his sense of possibility. Many things could happen in the course of an unfettered day in New York.

He walked down the avenue at a brisk clip, taking in the store windows and scanning the crowds for expensively dressed, lushly built women whom he might migrate into his fantasies. New York women, he already knew, were some of the most beautiful in the world. The intricately festooned windows at Saks gave him an excuse to linger while throwing sidelong glances at a leggy redhead wearing a fur coat and tall, tobacco-colored crushed suede boots. He stopped briefly to check out the skaters at Rockefeller Center, then headed downtown, taking a zig-zag route away from the thickest throng of shoppers and tourists.

Suddenly, about twenty-five feet ahead of him, a tall woman emerged from a doorway and joined the stream of foot traffic down Madison. She must have been six feet tall and had long, flowing black hair. As she turned, Baza caught a glimpse of high, sculpted cheekbones and deep red lipstick. He quickened his step, weaving through a sea of black and gray overcoats.

Now, just a few feet behind her, he could see that she wore a tight black leather skirt and sky-high heels beneath her short, puffy jacket. Her legs were long with well-defined calf muscles, like a dancer's, wrapped in silky pantyhose.

In the novel *Candide*, Voltaire wrote, "the nose has been formed to bear spectacles, thus we have spectacles. Pigs were made to be eaten, therefore we eat pork. Legs are visibly designed for stockings—and we have stockings."

He followed at a discreet distance as she turned up 39th toward Fifth, passed the Library with its iconic lions, and went into Lord & Taylor. Baza thought, *this is the kind of shopping I don't mind.*

Her allure was overwhelming. He followed her from aisle to aisle, feigning interest in some merchandise as she stroked a counter display of filmy scarves. Her long fingernails were the same deep scarlet as her lips; her thick lashes fluttered as she draped a chiffon animal-print scarf around her neck. Catching a glimpse of Baza in the mirror, she replaced the scarf, swished her hips and stepped onto the escalator, revealing the high, taut curve of her derriere with each step.

In a state of high excitement, Baza shadowed the Vixen, as he nicknamed her, while she meandered through racks of expensive designer clothing. She turned and looked straight at him for just an instant, then moved on with a flicker of a smile playing over her lips. He busied himself with a display of cashmere sweaters, pretending he was buying gifts for his mother or sister. Suddenly she appeared at his shoulder, leaned toward his ear, and whispered in a smoky alto voice, "Well, aren't you adorable...wouldn't it be easier if you just said hello?"

Baza blushed, knocked over a stack of sweaters with a nervous sweep of his arm, and blurted out, "You are so beautiful."

"Do you know what I am?" she asked. Her makeup gave her skin an airbrushed perfection under the fluorescent overhead lights.

"Yes, you are a gorgeous woman."

The woman put her hand on Baza's shoulder.

Just then a matronly shop clerk in her 60s seemed to step out of nowhere. She gave the woman a sharp look, and she immediately dropped her hand, though her eyes still lingered on Baza.

The clerk cleared her throat. "Can I help you, young man?"

"Oh, I was just looking for something...for my sister," he mumbled.

"I'd be happy to help you with that. What did you have in mind?" she asked, softening her tone.

The Vixen slipped away. Feeling trapped by the clerk and panicked in his confusion, Baza darted away, vaulted down the escalator, and fled into the sanctuary of the men's restroom. He had felt an unmistakable stirring as he trailed his quarry. Now, as he imagined what lay beneath that tight black leather skirt, he mushroomed firm and hard. His cheeks burned as he pulled his coat around him.

At that moment, Baza plunged into a recurring internal debate over his sexual preferences. Was he, like his father's friend, the General, one of those men who secretly lusted for his own kind?

He came to realize it was more complicated than that. His sexual preferences resided more in a grey area than within any traditional black or white interpretation of straight or gay. What aroused his sexual appetites was the image of the female with her gifts wrapped in an aura of glamour. The high heels and silky clothes, the curvy rump, the makeup, jewelry, and perfume—it was the *accouterments* that moved him to crave the flesh beneath. If the woman he desired was anatomically a man, it did not lessen his excitement. On the contrary, transsexuals like the Vixen, who manufactured their femininity, would prove to be the ones that most fueled his fantasies. They were like exotic hothouse flowers, all perfume and lush blossoms. Next to them, ordinary women were plain field daisies.

By the time Baza left his comfortable life in Honduras to study in the United States, he had also absorbed his father's expectations that he not only succeed in business, but help to enlarge the family's interests. Restless whenever he wasn't actively working on some business scheme, the elder Baza was counting on his son to help him unearth new opportunities in the vast reaches of the United States. There, he knew, marvelous new technologies and financial wizardry were combining to create a new order of wealth and prosperity. Baza needed to stay focused on his path in order to accomplish all that was expected of him. There was no room for the grey area.

3

In spite of his seven-figure salary and Connecticut estate, Big Bird could never quite shake his Midwestern roots. Loud, bombastic, and habitually overconfident, he resembled in many ways an overgrown high school boy on the make.

"Hey Baza, check out my new iPhone app," he demanded, as he tapped on the device and thrust it in front of Baza's face. The image of a beer stein slowly filling up with virtual beer appeared on the iPhone's screen. Big Bird then jerked the iPhone away from Baza and tilted it towards his mouth, ending the performance with a loud belch.

Big Bird had never gotten past his childhood love for novelties. He carried a fake Brad Pitt California Driver's License procured in Times Square, and would often bring out a magic trick or two in the course of a meeting. His colleagues at Moody's thought this behavior embarrassing and unprofessional, but Big Bird brought in the big bucks, so they joined in the laughter at his antics.

Michael Aloysius Mayberry was born and raised in Carlinville, Illinois, home to roughly 5,000 souls at the time of his birth in 1952;

nearly half a century later, the 2000 census listed its population as 5,685. The town is a four or five-hour drive from Chicago, but just 12 miles off Route 66, 40 miles from the Mississippi River, and 45 miles from Springfield, Illinois, where a young Abraham Lincoln practiced law. Tourist literature calls the area "Lincoln Land."

The Mayberry's were big shots in a small town, something Big Bird desperately wanted to remedy. From a young age, he dreamed of conquering London, New York and Hong Kong.

He succeeded in climbing higher than any of his classmates at Sacred Heart High School could have imagined. He headed up the entire sales program at Moody's, a senior position with a base salary as high as $2 million a year, plus bonuses.

While it may not have been obvious to someone from the outside, Moody's had become a sales-driven profit machine. The company had three major competitors, but with annual revenues north of $5 billion, Moody's was the clear market leader. What's more, it fought hard to wrest every possible point of market share from its rivals.

It was Big Bird's job to see that Moody's stayed number one.

Discipline was something he had learned a long time ago. For years, starting from the age of six, he got through the interminable Sunday Mass at St. Mary's by closing his eyes and pretending to pray while counting to 3,600. If his pacing was right, he finished counting just as the hour-long Mass drew to a close.

The main thing Big Bird absorbed from his childhood was a relentless hunger for bettering his circumstances. Coming out of the Depression and World War II, and planted in a backward, rural region with a family of five to provide for, his parents aspired to modernity, money and success.

For them, driving a pickup was taboo, the unmistakable mark of a rube, while being hooked up to the city water system was a sign of prestige. They ate their corn and beans out of a can, even though they were surrounded by hundreds of acres of corn and bean fields. Technically, the family's address was Rural Route 4, but they always listed it as 1110 E. Main Street.

The family business, Mayberry's, consisted of three storefronts awkwardly combined into the town's sole "department store," the place where locals bought ready-to-wear for those occasions when they weren't driving farm equipment or canning vegetables. Big Bird's father, Patrick, ran the business, and every child over the age of 12 was expected to put in time there. But it was his mother who drove the store's success.

One of nine Depression babies, Julia Frances Kilpatrick Mayberry grew up with a natural ability to cajole, fib, and charm, if that's what it took to get what she wanted. In addition to functioning as the store's buyer, training sales staff, and ruling over displays, she was a sales juggernaut who never let up until the customer walked out, parcel in hand. Whenever business was slow, Julia was brought in to boost volume and light a fire under the other salespeople.

It was she who taught Big Bird how to sell. She'd begin with that big Irish smile, then unleash a slow, steady barrage of compliments that were extravagant but never over the top. "Oh my, with your figure, that dress is going to stop traffic," she was fond of cooing. At a certain point, she would put her right foot forward in the "ready" position and switch to a posture of total deference. Without pause, her attention focused on the customer, she would continually nudge the sale forward until the wallet was unzipped and the money was in the register.

If the sale was a big-ticket item and one of her children happened to be nearby, she would wink at him, as a signal that things were looking up. Each sale meant meat in the freezer, a new dishwasher, college tuition. Each sale confirmed that the future was bright and all things were possible.

Despite the influence of his mother, his paternal grandfather, Seamus Mayberry, was the only family member who had experienced great success.

Seamus was born in 1912, in the southern Irish town of Cork, to the hapless wife of an alcoholic plumber. By the time he was 12 and already tired of living in grinding poverty with his mother and five brothers and sisters, he resolved to escape to the U.S. no matter what it took.

As soon as he turned 16, he made his way to Manchester and began haunting the docks, looking for work. He soon landed a job in the boiler room of a steamer bound for New York. For working a 10-hour shift, he received free passage, two meals, and 50 cents a day.

Within three days after landing in New York, he was hawking newspapers on the street. He soon hired younger boys to work for him, and spent his time scouting out street corners with ample traffic and little competition. Once he had saved $300, he bought a train ticket and headed west, getting off in Carlinville on the advice of a fellow traveler who owned the town's local dry goods store. The man had been so impressed by Seamus's eagerness that he offered him the job of stock boy on the spot.

When the store's owner died a few years later, Seamus bought the business from his widow, married a local girl, and branched out into other enterprises. He created a small town dubbed Mayberryville. He bought homes built on land to the west of town that was set to be flooded by the Army Corps of Engineers for $1 each. He then leased barges to float the houses down the river to St. Louis.

He also created one of the first discount stores, "The House of a Thousand Bargains," where prices were so low that people flocked there from a hundred or more miles away. He was an entrepreneur and a solid businessman known for flinty aphorisms such as, "a soft heart equals a soft head."

Wal-Mart could have been the Mayberry family destiny. All of the Mayberry clan seemed to have retail in their blood: Seamus's father, Aunt Marie, Uncle Jack and Uncle Dale. But things didn't work out that way. Seamus's four children went their independent ways, running their own stores, never leveraging their collective wisdom. They became sibling competitors who talked about joining forces, but never did. Life moved too quickly for them to huddle with a single purpose.

Just that year, 30 years after his grandfather's death, Big Bird earned $2 million a year in base salary and bonuses of $3.5 to 4 million. He seemed to represent the pinnacle of the clawing, scheming, expectations and hopes of the entire Mayberry clan.

Wasn't that kind of success what every Mayberry had sought? Wasn't it all about hitting the jackpot of fame and fortune?

But Big Bird still didn't feel that he'd arrived. Being a big fish in the small pond of Carlinville was not so difficult. Being a big fish in Silicon Valley, San Francisco or New York, required another level of luck, savvy, and ambition.

When Big Bird took a business trip to China and saw the women running the dozens of shops lining the Great Wall, it instantly called to mind his mother's techniques. The Chinese women aggressively pitched their wares, repeating "a dollah, a dollah, only cost a dollah, you buy for one dollah" over and over again. They knew how to wear you down, just like his mother did.

When Big Bird got to Wall Street, he built his book of business using the techniques of the family matriarch. She would say anything it took, including employing outright lies, to encourage and cultivate her "whale" customers, the rich women of the town who shopped for amusement and would buy almost anything she recommended. She called them "whales" because she'd read that's how Las Vegas card dealers referred to their high rollers.

Big Bird used the same term for his banking customers, who stood to make hundreds of millions of dollars by packaging up huge batches of mortgages and offloading them to investors. For the bankers, a decent rating from Moody's was the Good Housekeeping Seal of Approval—the credibility they needed to grease the transactions. Otherwise they had nothing but false promises to sell. Big Bird landed all the whales on Wall Street, persuading them to throw their business to Moody's, just as his mom had reeled in all the free-spending women of the town.

He had the magic touch, knowing exactly when and where to push and when to step back. Big Bird could turn a glass vase into crystal, a patent pending into an investment opportunity, an unrated bond into a money machine.

With his four rambunctious boys, even-tempered Midwestern wife, and 4,600-square-foot estate home in Greenwich, Connecticut, Big Bird was as steeped in domestic bliss as anyone on Wall Street. His job was lucrative and his family was secure. He believed that life was good, and he had the means to live it to the fullest.

Even with the boys and their pandemonium, he saw his home not as an oasis of serenity—but a refuge from his life as a Wall

Street super-salesman. Big Bird spent almost every waking moment angling to curry favor or rack up brownie points with some middle manager at Merrill Lynch, Goldman Sachs, Morgan Stanley or Lehman Brothers. Part of his job was to know exactly who was in charge of picking bond analysts in each shop. The bankers had four rating agencies to choose from; Big Bird was supposed to make sure they picked Moody's.

He cajoled, entertained, and sent lavish gifts. He got inside the heads of his sales targets, learning where they lived, how they thought, and what excited them in life. He pursued every deal, every client and every new opportunity with the same obsessive enthusiasm. Failure was not an option.

Theoretically, the banks distributed their ratings assignments evenly among the four firms based on some rotation scheme. But in practice, there was plenty of room for the banks to play favorites, and for Moody's to go after the big deals and big fees for itself.

Big Bird's sales strategy was simple. He'd tell clients, "Go ahead and send the small deals to Fitz, but send the big deals to me." Fees were based on a fixed, supposedly negotiable commission—a straight percentage of the deal, just like real estate commissions and mortgage brokers' fees.

A $2 billion deal brought in four times the revenue of a $500 million offering, but took almost the same amount of work. In rapidly rising markets, like the one for U.S. housing, that kind of fee structure operated as a self-priming money machine. What's more, appreciation of an asset class has a way of distracting attention from questions of its true costs and value. For Big Bird, it also had a way of distracting him from his family, and his wife was on a continual quest to alert him of dates he was supposed to remember, like his kids' birthdays.

What Big Bird didn't know was how to appreciate what he had. His father was the kind of person who found contentment in an easy chair and a glass of beer at the end of the day. He was satisfied with his accomplishments and grateful for the family's middle-class comforts. But Big Bird had the same restless, striving ambition as his mother and great-grandfather. He never stopped seeking more.

4

Baza was scheduled to meet his on-again, off-again girlfriend Kate, for dinner at the Gramercy Tavern. He realized, with a jolt, that since meeting Trina he hadn't thought of Kate once. Kate Stapleton was the sister of his old colleague from Silicon Valley, Tim Adams. Tim introduced them via a blind date a few years back and they dated for a few months before Baza decided to move back to New York to pursue a more high-flying finance career, which had been somewhat blown off course by the job at the Mayor's Office.

They had never formalized their relationship, much to Baza's relief, yet whenever he saw Kate, he was always left with the intrinsic knowledge that the easy camaraderie couldn't last and she would eventually want and demand more from him.

She was flying in from San Francisco late that afternoon, ostensibly on business, but she had texted before taking off, asking Baza to make time for her so they could catch up. He figured this meant that their on again off again affair might be gearing up for another round.

Baza also knew that ultimately Kate wanted marriage material, which was why their liaison originally wound down after a few months when he couldn't deliver on the commitment she was really hoping for. He wondered how long this dance would go on. He felt a slight pang of guilt, as knew that ultimately all roads led to disappointing her again. At the same time, he enjoyed her dynamic conversation and the companionship of a warm body to sleep next to. He reassured himself with the reminder that she was an adult and we all take our own risks. He just wished he could find a way to feel more for her. Maybe if he just tried harder?

He walked into Gramercy Tavern, their favorite spot when she came to town, to find her already sitting at the bar, her bag holding a stool for him amidst the crowded after work hubbub. Kate was a striking woman, at least 5'10", with narrow angular features and white-blonde hair, which was usually pulled back into a low ponytail. Her skin seemed to glow with a dew-kissed California sheen. He kissed her on each cheek by way of greeting.

"Kate, you look fantastic."

"Well, thanks, Baza. You look...a little stressed actually." She gazed at him with genuine concern.

"Oh, just working too many hours as usual." He waved it off. "California keeps treating you better and better."

"It's the regular surfing. You know I'm an addict."

"I know. It's hard to imagine you anywhere else."

"Can't be that hard. I'm an East Coast girl at heart, remember. I will probably end up here." She played with the rim of her water glass, drawing circles around it with her forefinger until she elicited a low hum.

"I doubt you'd ever really be happy here." Baza tried to steer the conversation back to safety.

"It all depends on the circumstances." She smiled suggestively at him.

"All I can do is take life as it comes these days."

"Of course, I totally get that." They drank and ordered dinner at the bar. Baza struggled to modulate his drinking. He felt compelled to drink to convince himself that he could continue to push the encroaching thoughts of Trina out of his mind.

He drained his Sambuca a little too quickly. "Shall we get a cab?"

"Yes, let me go to the ladies' room." She excused herself, which left Baza the opportunity to check his phone. He had a message from Trina, but decided not to click on it until later.

He paid the bill and waited for Kate by the front door. When she came out, she looked flushed, as if she had rouged her cheeks a bit more. He didn't pause to question the origin of her state, just ushered her out of the restaurant with a hand on the small of her back, like the dutiful half-boyfriend he was. It was a familiar drill, this façade of normative dating behavior, designed to show the world just how mainstream he really was. They would go back to his place and have serviceable sex, a couple more Scotches, before falling into a haze of fitful sleep, which would then be repeated for the next two to three nights until she left town.

For most Honduran immigrants, the path to the United States was a long, circuitous one fraught with hardship and even peril. For Baza, it was a straight shot through the marble halls of academia. An honors student at the American School of Tegucigalpa, the top prep school in Honduras, he applied in his senior year to four top-ranked U.S universities and one in the U.K.: Harvard, Yale, Stanford, Dartmouth, and Oxford. Though initially wait-listed by Stanford, he ended up being accepted to all five,.

His counselor at the American School, Jose Barzelatto, praised Stanford, his father favored Harvard, and his mother said, "You decide."

He chose Dartmouth. Baza liked the idea of attending a historic private college with a big reputation and a small student body. Established in 1769, Dartmouth was the *alma mater* of Daniel Webster, a figure Baza admired for his eloquence as an orator and his courage as a statesman. The college had just 6,000 students and Baza found the small-town atmosphere of Hanover, New Hampshire to be congenial.

Baza had attended the American School of Tegucigalpa from the age of four. Founded in 1946, it is a private, co-educational institution that instructs the children of elite Honduran families and well-to-do ex-pats, mostly from the U.S. and U.K. The school has a longstanding and well-deserved reputation for rigorous, yet caring instruction, which dovetailed perfectly with the educational ideals of the Ponce family.

Academically, Baza was well prepared for Dartmouth. From his earliest school days, he had been a serious, disciplined student. Thanks to his teachers and his appetite for American pop culture, he was also nearly as fluent in English as in his native tongue.

Yet in other ways, Baza found his first year on campus to be more difficult than he had expected. Although he had been raised to feel special, his pedigree now felt insignificant. The American students he had known at his school in Honduras were mostly from families in the upper echelons of the diplomatic corps; they were well off without being truly wealthy. In contrast, many of his Dartmouth classmates were the privileged offspring of families that had earned vast fortunes in the boom years of the 1980s and '90s. Coming from Honduras, where the oligarchy was defined more by class and strict observance of convention than by money, Baza couldn't help feeling intimidated by the sheer scale of American wealth.

Fortunately for Baza, he entered Dartmouth in 1990, at the moment when what might be called "ethnic chic" took hold in American culture. This was about the time it became fashionable for affluent American high-school and college students to spend their school breaks helping to build houses or staff medical clinics in the impoverished villages of Asia, Africa, or Central America.

By the end of his freshman year, Baza felt a new sense of approbation and interest from the other students he met. "You're from Honduras? Wow, that's really cool," they'd say. "I spent two weeks in Guatemala last year; I just *love* the people down there."

Increasingly, Baza came to see that being a well-to-do immigrant who spoke perfect English and knew gringo mannerisms could be an advantage, especially with the blond co-eds his exotic dark looks attracted. He thought back gratefully to Florence Abbott, the well-bred nanny his parents had imported from London to help ground him and his sister, Veronica, in English language and culture. At the breakfast table, their nanny would offer extra dollops of honey to the child who could perfectly recite a passage from Chaucer or Shakespeare.

Baza also gained a certain standing among his peers from his surprising facility with mathematics. Although Latins are not generally known for their grasp of differential equations or nonlinear analysis, it was in his math classes that Baza really shone.

During his first year at Dartmouth, Baza considered majoring in urban planning with a focus on economic development. He had left home with visions of returning to Honduras and helping to bring his poor, backward country into the 21st century.

But as he excelled in his mathematics courses and even won several prizes in regional math competitions, Baza gravitated more and more to math and its financial applications. Gaining expertise in finance, he realized, might be the way he could help re-invent the Honduran economy, which had remained dependent on small-scale agricultural, livestock, and mining operations since the 19th century. Studying finance would also equip him to help expand the family's fortunes, in accordance with his father's deepest wish.

Baza's intellectual hero and mentor at Dartmouth was Professor Robert Stangler, who combined finance and philosophy in a way the young Honduran found inspiring. The more he listened to Professor Stangler, the more Baza became intrigued with the concept of financial leverage and how it could be enlisted to accomplish great things with relatively modest resources.

"Leverage is the bridge between the assets you have and what you want to create," the professor would say, warming to his topic as he paced back and forth before his students in the stadium-style lecture hall. "We see debt as a necessary tool for building major public works, and even for buying a three-bedroom bungalow. So why should leverage be a dirty word? Would we have the pyramids, the city of Paris, or the Golden Gate Bridge without it? Of course not!"

As voluble as he was brilliant, Professor Stangler could lecture for hours, without notes, on credit markets, approaches to structuring debt, and the benefits and risks of financial leverage. He had the kind of mind that was able to find linkages between the mechanisms of finance and any other human endeavor. Huckleberry Finn, FDR, rap music, genetic research—no matter what the topic was, he found some novel way to connect the dots.

These flights of intellect enthralled Baza, who could now envision himself as a financial architect, using his skills to build a better life for his countrymen in a modernized, re-energized Honduras. He knew that the creative use of financial leverage had made America the richest country on the planet. He couldn't help imagining how it could transform his own small nation.

Stangler was also an expert on economic bubbles and the dynamics that create them, which he equated with a lynch mob mentality. As he described it, the trouble begins when enthusiasm for an asset builds to the point where it becomes self-validating and self-reinforcing. The result is a kind of delusional groupthink that takes on a life of its own, overpowering the will of any single individual. Just as otherwise law-abiding individuals can find themselves marching on a local jail, grabbing a prisoner and stringing him up, rational people may become so enthused about buying real estate or technology stocks that they discard their own better judgment.

The speculative mania for tulips in the 17th century, the South Sea bubble in the late 19th century, the U.S. stock market crash of 1929, skyrocketing Japanese asset prices in the early 1990s—as he preached on the pitfalls of investing based on emotion, Professor Stangler could cite these turning points chapter and verse

"When you get to Wall Street, Baza—because I know you will—be careful never to get caught up in the trends that excite everyone else," Professor Stangler cautioned his student. "That's the fundamental flaw in the Street's analysis. When the big-money guys get on board with something, their enthusiasm is contagious. The analysts are so pumped up by the collective excitement, they forget to look critically at the reasons behind it...and that's when things get really dangerous," he warned.

Years later, Baza would wistfully think back to his teacher's words.

5

In June 1994, Baza graduated from Dartmouth with honors. Many of his classmates were packing their bags for Europe or some more exotic locale, taking a break before plunging into the real world. Baza had a different plan.

He packed his books and belongings into his red 1992 Mercedes 230S Coupe and drove west, traveling 10 or 12 hours a day by the fastest interstate routes. Although his friends and family urged him to take the opportunity to "see America," he skipped the scenic views and tourist stops. Baza's destination was Silicon Valley, and he was eager to arrive.

Professor Stangler, Baza's mentor, adviser, and cheerleader through his last two years at Dartmouth, had often spoken of this brave new world where innovation was as focused on finance as on technology. On a single stretch of Sand Hill Road in Menlo Park sat the largest concentration of venture capital talent and resources in the country.

But what drew Baza wasn't just the piles of cash needing a place to roost. It was the freewheeling, pioneering spirit of the place. The

VC firms there weren't content to invest their capital and make a 20 or 25% annual return when they went to market with the IPO, the initial public offering of stock in a promising new firm. They were experimenting with new kinds of debt instruments they could layer on top of their equity investments in start-up technology firms—that is, vehicles for leveraging their leverage. Besides, Baza's father was looking to him for new ways to grow and modernize the family business. He was a man with a mission.

Told of Baza's plan, Professor Stangler exclaimed, "Good for you; that's what I'd be doing if I were your age now," adding a warning: "Don't ever forget that the combination of debt and innovation can create wonderment, or folly." But to Baza's way of thinking, there was no better place on earth to plumb the possibilities of financial engineering.

He was not alone. The technology sector was growing at a phenomenal rate, driven in large part by the commercialization of the Internet. With processing power and data storage getting cheaper every year, technology was also being applied to transform traditional industries and small businesses alike.

It was no wonder that some of the top graduates of Ivy League business schools were turning their backs on Wall Street and beating a path to Silicon Valley. They tended to be the brilliant iconoclasts and rebels who shunned the idea of business as usual—visionaries who focused less on amassing untold riches than on changing the world. If they became fabulously wealthy in the process, well, that was part of the magic of Silicon Valley. With the right financial framework, one good idea could spawn a whole new industry.

Baza's decision to pick Silicon Valley was cemented during his last semester at Darmouth, when he heard a guest lecture by Hugh Florence, an executive at Intel, and Ward Hansen, a professor at Stanford's School of Business. It was their description of the business culture that grew and flourished in the Valley that captured his imagination.

"Anything can be tried in the Silicon Valley and there is plenty of capital to fund it," explained Hansen. "Investors leverage financial equity against the possibilities of great ideas and the energy of smart human capital."

The concept of leveraging an idea for an unpredictable reward fascinated the mathematician in Baza. How could something so ephemeral prompt smart people to plunk down millions in hard cash? It defied all the quantitative analytical methods he'd been taught. If you were investing in an industry that didn't yet exist, there was no basis for calculating a rate of return. This kind of finance was all art, and very little science.

"That is not a business, it is a flight of fancy, a *sueño*," his father often said when Baza told him of some new technological marvel about to be hatched. But while the elder Baza questioned the very reason for the Valley's existence, he was also curious about the ways his son might help the family diversify its holdings with faster-growing U.S. enterprises. He was wise enough to know his son might be able to see the world in ways he couldn't.

"That's fine, you keep studying leverage, and we will leverage your brain back home when you are done," he would say.

Baza landed a job at Benner Finland, a top-tier VC firm that focused on enterprise software as well as health care and energy technologies. The firm was an early backer of Apple Computer and later became one of the biggest investors in Internet companies.

As a junior analyst, Baza's first task was to take a critical look at the business plan submitted by two Stanford graduates who wanted to build an online stock trading business on the AOL platform.

"Imagine being able to trade stocks on AOL any time of day or night, instead of trading phone calls with your stockbroker," said Tim Adams, founder of the fledgling company, and Kate's brother. "No brokers, no forms, no paying the middleman—just a marketplace where you can get the same information as the Wall Street guys and buy or sell stocks anytime you want."

Baza politely threw a hail of questions at Adams. "Where do you get the data? How do you protect the privacy of investor information? How do you collect trading fees? Is it safe? How does it scale? Can the bulge bracket firms stop you? How do you defend your patent?"

Adams was quick on his feet. He was the model of a second-generation Silicon Valley entrepreneur, Baza thought. Intel, Microsoft, and Apple were the old guard. Here was someone who could look beyond the building blocks of technology and see where the information highway was leading. These new titans of the Valley were creating a consumer phenomenon that would reshape both commerce and society.

At the time, however, it was hard to see how Adams' vision could be realized. His firm's financial forecasts were shaky, at best, and the business model he proffered was half-baked. Nevertheless, his ideas around online financial transactions fascinated young Baza. The elegance and simplicity of the model made him smile.

Fast forward ten years to the mortgage-backed securities desk at Moody's: Baza would often criticize financial models for being overly complex. He also believed that reliance on a black box—a financial engine whose workings were kept hidden from human eyes—was usually a sign of a flawed underlying model.

When he was younger, Baza was an idealist, in that he believed investments should be transparent and risk should be explained in ways that investors could actually understand. Eventually he learned that the confusion created by black boxes and complicated models was an intentional part of the sell. If you made it all a blur, you could charge more, boost your profits, and stay in business longer. The less your customer or investor understood what you were doing, the more potentially valuable it was. The smokescreen was also a barrier to competitors.

But while he was in Silicon Valley, Baza bought into its brand of hope. Coming from Honduras, a land of limited prospects and seemingly intractable woes, he reveled in the optimism exuded by California entrepreneurs.

"In Honduras, if we see the light at the end of a tunnel, we look for another tunnel," he told his manager, Michael Bullington, a BF partner who had studied economics at Cal and earned his MBA at Stanford. A lanky marathon runner, Bullington drove fast cars and went helicopter skiing on his rare vacations.

Baza's boss encouraged him to stay focused on innovation and opportunity. "Smart people with capital can change the world," he said. "Wall Street wears you down; the Valley revs you up."

It turned out that Baza was perfectly positioned not only to explore new frontiers in investment banking, but also to learn first-hand about economic bubbles. He was personally involved with the financing of Netscape, the launch of Expedia and the first business plan for Google. In other words, the young math whiz was there for the technology boom and then watched it turn into the dot-com bust. This is what propelled him to business school at NYU, to see if there was something he could learn about business and human nature that could help people stave off these bouts of mania that led to such busts.

When he eventually left California, it was not before he saw how a fever for ideas and dreams could whip up smart, well-educated people. Their enthusiasm was like a forest fire so huge it generated its own wind, burning through anything in the way. His intention had always been to go to New York, gather another degree and some East Coast experience, and then return to the land of sunshine, and what he deemed as a more civilized existence than the mania of Wall Street.

Since meeting Trina weeks before, she had appeared in his dreams on several occasions as a welcoming presence that beckoned and then faded out of reach. When her image began creeping into his daydreams, he knew his resistance was crumbling.

After three weeks, he finally tried calling her. Not wanting to leave a message on her answering machine, he called several times before he heard the voice of Trina herself in a sultry "hello." She seemed surprised and pleased to hear from him, offering to entertain him at her apartment. She gave an address on Rivington Street on the Lower East Side.

On the way to Trina's, he stopped in for a couple of snorts at Lucky Cheng's, just to take the edge off. Mick was bragging about his holdings in tech stocks, particularly one company, called Textronics, that was trading on the Canadian penny exchange and was poised to make its investors a fortune. The firm was touting a new automobile ignition system that promised to sweep all its competitors away.

"Where did you find out about Textronics?" Baza asked Mick warily. Baza suspected a bar patron had peddled Bob the idea, hoping he'd spread the word among Lucky Cheng's well-heeled patrons. It was an old trick, and one that often worked. Mick said his portfolio was up $45,000 since the first of the year and was sure to go still higher. Baza told him he'd be smart to cash in most of his gains while he was ahead. Mick demurred and changed the subject to golf. After chatting about his job, his father, and Mick's love life, Baza left to keep his assignation.

The temperature had dropped almost 10 degrees since Baza entered the bar. He hailed a cab, then stuffed his hands in the pockets of his blue blazer to keep warm. As they approached Rivington Street, he could feel the pulse pounding in his neck. He had the driver drop him about a block from Trina's address. He walked up Rivington to a nondescript mid-rise that looked to be from the 1960s. The glass door was covered with a wrought-iron security grill.

He rang the bell, and in a moment, the door buzzer sounded as the latch released, letting him push his way in. "I hope no one sees me," he thought. His preference for TS women was one secret he wanted to keep that way. But in a moment of self-awareness, he realized that it was the sense of danger that brought his excitement to a fever pitch. For Baza, it was the wrapper around an experience that mattered. He was one of those men who always found the veil more intriguing than the face beneath.

As he climbed five flights of squeaky stairs, he held his breath against the strong smell of cooking onions and garlic. Muffled voices could be heard inside several apartments. He found number 507 and knocked on the door.

"Just a minute," Trina called in a sexy girl-boy voice. She opened the apartment door with caution, then reached for Baza's elbow and pulled him inside. She quickly bolted the door and wrapped her arms around him, pressing her mouth to his. The feeling of her tongue sliding over his lips and thrusting into his mouth made him dizzy. He stepped back for a moment to look her over. Dressed in a silky flowered kimono that was loosely belted around her trim waist, Trina was pretty, sexy and flirtatious.

Without pause, they went back to kissing, stumbling into her tiny apartment and falling to the velour couch in the living room. He reached into her kimono, wanting her breasts, but she denied him. "You can have anything else you want," she promised.

"Here, Mr. Baza, you can look at my legs," she crooned. "Don't you think these are the most beautiful legs in all of New York? Would you like to kiss them and feel my stockings."

The studio apartment was tastefully decorated in neutral colors and had an entire wall of mirrors, making it feel more spacious than its 600 square feet.

The bed was a mattress on the floor, but it was appointed with a rich-looking bedspread and plush pillows.

"You just lie there, get comfortable and watch," she whispered as she struck a series of provocative poses, stroking her sex. Baza was mesmerized at first, then, as if in a trance, reached down into his pants and began rubbing himself. In less than a minute, he groaned with an explosive orgasm.

"Ohhh, Baza...why didn't you wait for me? You bad boy," she mock-scolded.

Baza recovered quickly and then, attempted to make small talk.

"How long have you lived here?

"Almost five years. It's not a palace exactly, but it works," Trina got up and went to get a drink. "Do you want some tea?"

"No, I'm good, thanks." Baza felt restless. He dressed quickly as she puttered in the tiny kitchen area. He slipped $300 under the napkin holder with the bills sticking out so she wouldn't miss it.

He stood behind her, his hands on her hips and kissed the back of her neck. "Thank you. I have to go."

"By Mr. Baza," she said, without looking back at him. He let himself out and trotted downstairs into the cool air and hailed another taxi back uptown. As he sat in the cab and watched the blocks whiz by, his imagination was running wild. He felt sure that he had been seen...that he was being followed or would be caught some other way. Beads of sweat broke out on his upper lip. It was not until he reached the Village and his ostensibly respectable life that he began breathing more easily.

Baza visited Trina four times over the next seven days. He felt like he was taking a huge risk every time he traveled downtown after work to see her. Whether it was real or imagined he couldn't be sure, but whatever it was, it was driving him to her like a magnet to metal filings.

Trina wore Opium by Yves Saint Laurent which he had first recognized as a scent worn by his mother many years ago. But on Trina it took on another life form. Baza knew enough about perfume to know that it smelled differently on different people, forming a unique confluence of olfactory experience based on an individual's pheromones. On Trina, Opium was an exotic and intoxicating scent which made Baza almost delirious with lust for her as soon as he smelled it on her neck.

She seemed to intrinsically know how to draw out Baza's anticipation, only revealing small parts of herself at a time. Baza stayed longer and longer each visit, eventually finding himself falling asleep at her place, waking up in the early hours of the morning, his head blurred and aching from whiskey. He would stumble out of her apartment, catch a taxi back home and stand under a long hot shower for an inordinately long time before finally getting dressed and getting himself into work. His brain was working overtime in machinations of self-incriminating diatribes the whole time.

That didn't stop him from making grand gestures towards Trina, becoming something of her knight in shining armor. During one whiskey-fueled night, lying next to her after sex and looking around her small studio, he found himself suddenly compelled by the idea that he needed to help her get on the property ladder while she still had a chance. He had already heard tales of her dodgy landlord who kept hiking the rent on her every six months.

"Have you thought of buying your own place?" Baza asked.

Trina just laughed. "That's funny. How is someone like me gonna get a mortgage? I work in cash."

"Depends on how much cash you have to put down." Baza traced her left leg with the tips of his fingers.

"I have some. I always wanted to get my own place. But you need a lot for that, right?"

"It really just depends." He paused, then found his lips moving before his brain had time to catch up. "I might be able to help you."

Trina propped herself up on her elbows and looked at him skeptically. "Really? You'd do that?"

"I want to help. You deserve to live in a better place than this."

She studied him for a minute then flopped back on the bed and turned away. "You're full of shit."

"What? No, I'm not. I mean it!" Baza pulled her into the curve of his body and inhaled the scent of her hair. "Let me make some calls. I'm going to help you find something and you'll end up paying less for a mortgage than you will for rent in this dump."

Trina didn't respond, but took his hand and pulled it closer into her body, encircling it with hers. He lay with her until he felt the steady, deep rhythm of her breathing and knew she was asleep. He gently untangled himself from her, dressed quickly, and left, hailing a cab back uptown. He didn't feel like going right home though. It was only 9:30 pm, not too late for another round. He decided to keep going past the Village and go to the bar at the Ritz, where he was likely to see a familiar face.

The bar was packed, but just as Baza entered, a gentleman vacated a seat at the south end of the bar, next to one panel of the restored Maxfield Parrish mural for which the bar was named. This panel of the celebrated mural depicted an entire group of courtiers giggling because the prince had just wet his pants.

He found himself seated next to two Russian women on one side and a handsome, distinguished-looking man with graying temples on the other side. Jacques, he learned, was from France and in town to attend functions at the United Nations. He was also staying at the St. Regis, which commanded $700 to $1,000 a night for a small room.

As Baza slipped into the conversation, he overheard one Russian woman, the glamorous one, whom the other one called Paulina, exclaiming "I always live for today!" Her big, freshly blow-dried blonde hair was laced with a hot pink grosgrain ribbon.

She was wearing an excessive amount of clanking jewelry, which looked to be real gold.

With its fitted waist and straight skirt, her deep blue dress had been well chosen to show off her figure, which was ample without being plump. Blooming from the right shoulder of the dress was a large white silk peony the size of a butter plate. She crossed and re-crossed her legs several dozen times in the next hour, giving anyone nearby a tantalizing mystery shot each time.

Her soft, high-pitched kitten voice and Russian accent gave her a sexual edge, even when she was talking about the weather.

"You say your name is Baza, are you from Spain? I lived in Spain once, I love Spanish men... Have you been to Tosa De Mar?

"No, I'm from South America, Brazil," he said, recalling his old school friend's saying about "strange cities, strange bars, telling lies to strange women."

Paulina's companion, Layla, smiled at the unfolding action. She was not a sexpot like her friend—she seemed more like a hanger-on, but hardly helpless. Her manner said, "Game on." Her English was terrible, but the universal language of sexual innuendo—winks, smiles, casual yawns and subtle arm move-ments—she had perfected.

The two Russian women put on a command performance. They were like a finely calibrated tag team of sexual predation. "Bravo," Baza thought, "Putin would be proud." Add in the French diplomat, and the group offered an irresistible mix of danger and possibility.

Most of Baza's friends could not understand why he traipsed uptown to frequent spots like the Ritz-Carlton, the King Cole Bar, the London Hotel and the Carlyle Hotel. That is not what 40-year-old men generally did. But he felt more comfortable there than he did competing with the smug hipsters downtown. More importantly, he gravitated towards older women, who were far more numerous in his uptown haunts.

For Baza, midtown hotel bars were an escape where he could usually turn up some interesting conservation and might find a bit of adventure. It was the aura of risk that piqued his interest, and dicey situations were not uncommon in these high-end bars. He had found that Russian women were often leading players in these dramas.

Knowing of Baza's proclivities, his friend Charlie Rutherford, a policeman whom he had met while playing soccer in Central Park, told him more than once, "You don't need to worry about crime in the streets of New York, it's the Russian women in high-end hotels you have to watch out for. They're the ones committing crimes against the likes of you."

Baza continued making conversational hay with the "live for today" line as the foursome consumed more alcohol and ate freely from the silver bowls of mixed nuts, olives and chips, which the bartender kept refilling.

After an hour, Baza did not like the way the scene was shaping up. It was obvious that the Russians had fixed on their marks. Jacques was to pair off with Paulina, while he was to be with Layla, with each couple going their separate ways. Paulina was the catch: She was very sexy and had that whiff of the danger he craved. He could see that the Frenchman not only shared his attraction to danger, but was also sufficiently drunk to pursue it without much regard for the consequences.

"Jacques, take me to Cartier on 55th and Fifth. I want to show you the Koh-I-Noor diamond. It's like nothing you have ever seen," Paulina purred in Jacques' ear as he seemed to lap up the attention. "It's 120 carats with a history going back 5,000 years. It's the largest cut diamond in the world."

Baza tried to give him a warning eye, just imagining what she would be ogling for him to buy for her, but Jacques was away and oblivious. Baza gave up and checked his phone again, as he had run out of small talk to make with Layla, whose limited English made even that difficult.

Baza wished his new French friend an agreeable adventure, but he also knew that the longer Jacques spent with the Russian woman on the make, the more likely he was to get into trouble.

"I'm going to have to leave you fine people, very early start tomorrow," he said, handing Jacques his business card, but not giving one to the Russians.

"Thank you, my friend. Please, I would like to meet this Big Bird you speak of. The French state pension fund is looking to expand its investments into the U.S. mortgage market"

"Absolutely, we'll make that happen," Baza said, as he leaned in and said in his ear, "Take good care of yourself," though he wasn't sure if he was overstepping his bounds with his new friend. Baza had a feeling it probably wouldn't make much difference either way, as Jacques was gunning his motors, fueled by alcohol and sex drive.

"Don't go, you party pooper," Paulina drawled, casting her eye on her friend to measure her disappointment at suddenly facing the end of the night without a catch.

"Sorry, ladies, duty calls. Don't get into too much trouble without me," Baza winked and made his escape, but not without picking up the check as his customary Mr. Big Shot gesture. He slipped downstairs to the restroom near the St. Regis hair salon. He looked in the mirror and said to himself, "You dodged another bullet; be grateful."

Baza stepped into a taxi waiting for a fare just outside the hotel and was back at his Village townhouse with 15 minutes, sweeping easily through late-night Manhattan streets. He was asleep as soon as his head hit the pillow, barely managing to kick off his shoes. Hus sleep was short-lived, however, as some time later he was awakened by the ringing of his phone, which he usually kept on silent.

He answered groggily and heard the Frenchman on the other end of the line. "Monsieur Baza, I am in urgent need of your advice."

"What happened?" He asked, expecting to hear the worst.

"I'm so sorry. I know this is a great deal to ask, as we only met this evening...but I would be most grateful if you could possibly come to see me at my hotel. I was robbed by the Russian women and don't know what to do next. I am afraid to tell anyone else."

Baza agreed to try to help him and said he'd be there soon. He stumbled into the bathroom and splashed cold water on his face. He called a car service to take him to the St. Regis and pulled himself together enough to be downstairs to get into the car within 15 minutes. His mind roiled with thoughts of what might have happened to poor Jacques. He was not surprised by the evening's outcome, nor by the Frenchman's call. They had connected well enough for him to realize that Baza would understand how he got into such a mess.

Long ago Baza had learned that the first step in being cleansed of your sins was to find some neutral third party who could relate to what you'd done and would extend the forgiveness you needed. Cabs were Baza's most common confessional unless, of course, the driver was Middle Eastern, in which case he did not expect understanding.

When he got to the St. Regis, he found that Jacques's room was on a V.I.P. floor that could only be accessed with a passkey. After a call to secure Jacques's permission, the bellman swiped the card, letting the elevator take Baza up to the 16th floor.

Jacques greeted him at the door, looking disheveled and wan. His tie was undone, his expression was grim, and his eyes were red.

"She robbed me at Cartier," he said. "How do you say, she 'clipped me' for a five-thousand-dollar watch; can you believe it?"

"Slow down, Jacques. Exactly what happened after I left? How did she rob you?"

"We went to Cartier to see that crazy diamond she kept talking about. She seemed to know the security guard there; I noticed how he smiled and let her in, even though she didn't have a printed invitation like the others who were coming in. It was a private event.

"We saw the diamond, and she was holding my arm, squeezing and stroking it…she kept talking all the time, 'live for today, live for today.'

"We looked around the store and she pulled me over to a case of gold watches, they were *trops chers*…very expensive. She kept pointing to one she especially liked, teasing me, "Why don't you show me you can live for today and buy me that watch?"

The Frenchman shook his head despairingly. "Why did I have so much to drink? It is not usually my way. I was also intoxicated with this Russian woman for some reason I cannot explain.

"I hesitated, of course, but she called over the clerk and said, 'This gentleman wants to buy me a watch. May we please see this one so I can try it on?'

"Like in a dream, I pulled out my business Amex card, the one from the Embassy, and bought her the watch. Then we arranged to meet for dinner after she freshened up. She promised to put on some special lingerie from Paris.

"She told me to be at the Bull and Bear in the Waldorf-Astoria in one hour; then we would go to the Country Restaurant at the Carlton. I made reservations and waited at the Bull and Bear for more than one hour. I was devastated...so I came back here and called you. I did not know what else to do." The Frenchman sat slumped as his voice trailed off.

Baza was momentarily silent. He was stunned by the gullibility of his new friend, who appeared so worldly and intelligent. But he could also relate to Jacques's buffoon-like behavior, and the way the Russian woman had virtually put him in a trance. She had not only convinced him that an intimate evening with her was worth $5,000, but she had also made him believe she would actually show up for their assignation.

Baza realized Jacques had no legal case against the mysterious Russian. He bought her a watch of his own accord, not at gunpoint. No crime had been committed, and it was no use to call the police. His only recourse was to stop payment on his Amex card, but he had signed the purchase receipt and could not return the watch. The Amex auditors would undoubtedly rule in favor of Cartier.

Explaining this to his boss was another matter.

Baza hatched a strategy of coming clean, at least partially so. He suggested that Jacques immediately contact the head of Embassy operations, saying that he had mistakenly used the wrong card while buying his wife a gift. He could then write the Embassy a personal check for the amount.

It was a five-thousand-dollar mistake, but not one that would not wreck his career or his marriage.

As Baza left the hotel room, Jacques had his head in his hands, repeating over and over again: *"Quel idiot! Je suis tellement stupide!"*

There is a right way to do wrong, thought Baza.

6

Baza's obsession with Trina grew alongside his growing concern about his role in the housing market bubble at Moody's, though one which he pushed down below the level of conscious thought every time it bobbed to the surface. Instead, he focused on how he could use his position to help Trina buy an apartment with enough cash down that she would be buffeted in a downswing of the market, should that come to pass as his intuition told him it would, however long he let it waft into his consciousness.

After his first month on the job, in October of 2005, he attended one of the many housing industry conferences, which were proliferating like mushrooms after a season of rain. Real estate values kept climbing, and the volume of mortgage-backed securities was rising so rapidly that the analysts and academics had to ask the question: Is it a boom, or a bubble?

One after the other, the expert panelists at the conference trotted out all the reasons why the smart money could expect the boom to continue. For starters, the U.S. population was projected to continue growing steadily for decades, thanks in no small part to immigration. An expected 148 million new residents by 2050 would add up to a lot of housing demand.

While Federal Reserve Chairman Alan Greenspan had come to regret his role in the nation's "irrational exuberance" over the stock market in the 1990s, the Fed had pushed interest rates to historic lows in an effort to keep recession at bay and showed little sign of reversing that policy. In a speech the previous year, Greenspan had also suggested that more use of adjustable-rate mortgages, which periodically reset to prevailing market rates, might help make homeownership more widely affordable.

Most compelling of all, the nation seemed to be swimming in a sea of prosperity. Baby Boomers were the richest generation in history and spent accordingly. The economy had pulled out of its post 9/11 doldrums, unemployment was trending downward, and consumer confidence was strong.

This was the message the crowd of housing developers, mortgage originators, and investors had come to hear. They were looking for smooth sailing ahead—not for red flags that might derail their plans and projections. The lone voices of dissent came from a handful of bloggers, who were quickly dismissed by industry insiders as amateurs and troublemakers.

A skeptic by nature, Baza saw the smug certainty of the housing market bulls as foolhardy. He knew enough about classic Greek plays to remember that hubris usually led to tragedy. Baza knew that in this scenario, the poisoned apple was high-risk, subprime mortgages—and his group was rating more and more loan packages stuffed with them.

Baza left the conference with few new facts, but what he'd heard deepened the sinking feeling in his gut. His intuition told him the boom was a house of cards—one that he himself was helping to prop up. His group continued to give triple-A ratings to mortgage packages that would turn to junk if home prices declined as little as 5 to 10 percent.

The thing was, Moody's bond rating models had no factor for a decline in home prices. That was the firm's dirty little secret. In Baza's mind, it was also a ticking time bomb.

But Baza knew how hard it would be to get anyone in a position of power to listen. The year 2005 was already shaping up to be the biggest on record for home sales, with more than seven million transactions. Everybody who stood to get a piece of the pie—mortgage lenders, bondholders, investment bankers, real estate agents, and homebuilders—were raking it in, and Moody's was no exception.

What's more, housing fever had spread to the population at large. Homeowners watched with glee as their real estate values inflated by the month, and many leveraged their paper wealth to finance remodeling, buy an investment property, or go on shopping sprees. Many of the nation's leaders, all the way up to the President, were cheerleaders, too, pointing to the boom as evidence of the country's economic strength.

It was a textbook case of what Charlie Munger, Warren Buffett's partner in Berkshire Hathaway, one of the most successful investment firms of all time, called "the Lollapalooza effect."

Baza remembered what Professor Stangler, his mentor at Dartmouth, had to say in his lecture on financial bubbles. "Periods of giddy optimism, when we most need thoughtful people to stand up and scream, 'You've all got it wrong, what's happening is destructive and bad, not good,' are precisely the times when it's most difficult to do that.

"Not only do you look crazy, everybody else thinks you're a killjoy, a downer who's just trying to wreck things for everybody else," the professor had warned. "Very few individuals have the courage it takes to stand up and confront the crowd."

Did he have the courage? Should he go to the mat for revising Moody's valuation model so that it at least allowed for the possibility of flat or declining home prices?

One of the speakers at the conference did say, "If the housing market changes, it will move like a large ocean liner, taking a long time to turn the other way."

Baza hoped that was true. If he were going to persuade the executives that adjusting the valuation model was the only prudent course, he was going to need a well thought out strategy and an airtight set of arguments.

The conference had wound up for the day and attendees were pouring out of the conference room into the hotel bar to wax rhapsodic about the gravy train they were all hitched to. It turned Baza's stomach and he didn't want to engage in shop talk with anyone after a long day of listening and schmoozing. He escaped the hotel and walked a few blocks before dipping into a small dark bar that seemed to be hosting a few lone drinkers and clandestine couples on barstools whispering into each other's ears.

Baza ordered a double Scotch, grabbed a cocktail napkin and started making notes.

Moody's was exactly the opportunity he had dreamed of while getting his degrees at Dartmouth and NYU. The compensation package, the benefits, and the potential for advancement—it all spelled "success."

Yet an internal conflict was grating at his insides. It had started eating away at him the last couple of weeks, he wasn't exactly sure how long. But maybe since he met Trina and his conviction grew that he could help her. At the same time, he was started to feel that his grand coup and vision was instead perhaps a teetering house of cards; that maybe, instead of all the value he was delivering for his adopted company he was getting up every morning and opting to be a part of what most Americans would call a Ponzi scheme. It was starting to settle low in his gut and gradually working its way up to his frame until he could feel the bile in his throat where it lodged itself much of the time.

All through college and his early work years in California he had prided himself on eating a healthy breakfast, something in the vein of egg whites and avocados with some intolerable kale choked down to assuage his guilt from cocktails the night before. Baza would hear his father's voice rattling in his brain—focus on keeping what you have, avoid unnecessary risks, be wary of supposed shortcuts to wealth—why did he think he could have it all? He thought that perhaps his dawning realization was just the price he was meant to pay for sitting in the lap of luxury.

As someone who valued analytical rigor, he knew logically that the risks of mortgage-backed securities were considerable, particularly if the housing market was to collapse. Never mind that few credible experts thought that was likely or even possible. For the most part, only a few bloggers on the fringe were putting the words "housing" and "bubble" together.

The trends seemed to validate the industry's optimism. The volume of mortgage-related CDOs was skyrocketing. In 2005, Wall Street pumped out $178 billion in mortgage and other asset-backed CDOs. By the next year, that figure had already reached $316 billion. With underwriting fees as high as one-half percent, the tidal wave of mortgage-backed offerings was just too big and too profitable to resist.

Baza's team was the focal point for the "due diligence" upon which Moody's based its credit ratings. Their job was to gauge the quality and risk of securities offerings by analyzing the underlying pools of mortgages. These could range from small groups of maybe 500 home loans worth $50 million to gigantic mortgage pools representing 10,000 loans worth $1 billion or more. Each pool had a code name that told you which lender had originated the loans— names like Frontier 1 and Yellow Road 2.

That morning, Baza was leading a bi-weekly team meeting where he was giving everyone a pep talk. After all, he was not yet about to let the chasm in his head and heart bleed into external reality yet. If ever.

"I'm sure you are all aware and I don't need to remind you of the ironclad law of Moody's business: while our assessments can't be divorced from reality—the firm's long-term success depends on keeping up our reputation for quality—the goal is to give each security the very best credit rating the team can justify.

"We all want 'sleep-easy-at-night' loans in the pool. Then everybody wins—the lenders, the underwriters, the investors, the homebuyers, and, of course, Moody's itself. Am I clear?"

Most of the heads in the room nodded. Baza knew that for most of his team, no one saw any reason to question their implicit marching orders. Then there was Melinda Glover, a 20-something working-class woman from Elizabeth, New Jersey. Her Rubenesque figure and soft, curly brown hair masked a will of steel. Baza would often find her being the last one to leave the office late at night. That day was no exception. He had stopped working on ratings a few hours earlier and was just trolling the real estate listings, looking for a gem in the rough for Trina and sending email inquiries to agents. His eyes were getting blurry and he had a pounding headache. He couldn't remember the last good night of sleep he had. He would try going to sleep without a nightcap tonight to see if that helped.

"Call it a night?" Baza suggested, walking past Melinda's desk and nodding at the wall clock that said 11:30 pm.

Melinda didn't even look up from her pad where she was scribbling figures. "You can. I'll finish this off." Baza appreciated her work ethic and he had heard her make several passing comments about not wanting to struggle like her working-class parents always had. He noticed that she would go to the mat for any policy that advanced the firm's fortunes, and thus her own. They were working in a climate where the team's compensation and bonuses were tied to productivity, as gauged by the number and dollar value of offerings processed. If you proved yourself able to turn ratings around in record time, so much the better.

"Where do you think this is all headed?" Baza asked an open-ended question because he was curious to see if Melinda was willing to cast any doubt on the work in front of them at this late hour. There was a pause as she took a moment to answer.

"You know, my Dad's mortgage used to be his piggy bank; he thought of his payments as a way to increase his equity and his savings," she said. "Now that he's refinanced, he uses it as a credit card. I tell him to be careful, but he doesn't listen. All I can do is grab onto the horns of the bull, and hold on for the ride. And that's what I intend to do."

"And I'm sure you will," Baza laughed.

"Go home, Baza. I can finish this."

"It's finished already, Melinda. Going over it four more times isn't going to change anything. Goodnight." Baza smiled wryly as he gathered his papers and called to reception to order a Lincoln Town Car to pick him up downstairs and take him home, the company policy for anyone who worked after 8 pm.

Just as he started to walk away, Melinda said, "I'm well aware we have no way of detecting fraud."

"Yup!" Baza replied.

"Most of these loans we look at have 'no stated income,' so we have no idea how much money the borrowers even make."

"For all we know, the names were gathered from some homeless shelter," Baza said.

"I know, I know. A deal could be a huge scam running right under our noses, and we'd never know it." She looked up from her spreadsheet and met Baza's gaze without blinking. "But I'm still buying my home in the Hamptons."

"I know you are," Baza said as he left and went downstairs to get his car.

He sat back in the plush seat of the Lincoln and watched lower Manhattan whiz by the window, as buzzing as ever, and thought about what would now be thought of as "the old days," when borrowers would have been required to make down payments of at least 20 to 30 percent and to whittle down the loan principal steadily. In many cases, they wouldn't have qualified for a home loan at all. But such strictures were going by the wayside in the current boom, with its heady combination of falling interest rates, rising home prices, and lending innovations such as interest-only loans. Baza couldn't square the reality—that many aspiring homeowners were not only able to purchase a home with zero down, but also to qualify for a substantial credit line in the bargain—with the more sage and timeless business practices he had learned from Professor Stangler at Dartmouth.

Whenever Baza started to feel the doubt rising about their work at Moody's he would then ask himself what he was doing criticizing the cash cow that was the answer to everything in his life that he felt he needed to escape from. Maybe if he just had enough money, he could make any potential problems that threatened his livelihood go away, and then he could just stop. Simple as that. Wasn't it? He wasn't so sure. He sometimes wondered if he might be an addict—not to drugs or booze, but to all this that supported his lifestyle and everything in it.

The Town Car pulled up in front of his building and he went upstairs and poured himself two fingers of single malt Scotch to clear his head and help him get to sleep, which had become such a habit of late he wasn't sure at this stage if he could sleep without it. He was exhausted yet wired. A horrible combination and completely counter-productive for achieving actual sleep. He lay there staring at the shadows of the city lights dancing on the wall of his bedroom. He thought about Trina, who had been saving for a down payment on her first home but was seemingly never able to get there because of the insane cost of living in this city. He decided if he couldn't fix the system, he was at least going to help the people he cared about profit from it. He had promised to help her find a place she could afford but hadn't made the calls yet. He wasn't sure which fear was holding him back: the fear of the overinflated market or the potential commitment his somewhat drunken promise entailed. At the same time, he wanted to be a man of his word. He told himself he would make some calls first thing in the morning.

7

The one person with whom Baza could speak freely about his misgivings was his deputy, Sandra Cherovich, a 32-year-old Harvard MBA who had migrated from Goldman Sachs when it became clear she wasn't deemed partner material.

It was Saturday morning and Baza was heading into the office. He rounded the corner in his neighborhood and ran straight into Sandra, coming out of the local yoga studio. He wasn't entirely surprised. She was rail-thin and an avowed vegan.

"Hey, you live in this neighborhood?" he was genuinely pleased to see her and was happy for any distraction from getting into the office.

"Baza! Yes, I do. How funny, you too, I'm gathering. Want to grab a coffee?"

"Absolutely." Baza replied, and they walked and talked until they got to the Starbucks on the corner.

"I realize you might not have expected it of me, but I've become a bit of a yogi. It's the only way I survive," Sandra laughed.

"Really? Maybe I should take up yoga," Baza said.

"Seriously, you might want to consider it. Before yoga, while I was still at Goldman, I was pretty unbearable—the kind of person who finished everyone else's sentences and would interrupt meetings to say, 'No, you're wrong.' You could say I've smoothed out my rougher edges by practicing *asanas* for an hour in the morning and an hour every night after work.

"Wow Sandra, that's impressive, I gotta admit."

"Which part? That I was such an asshole or that I practice asanas now?" she winked.

"Well both, actually," Baza replied.

"Fair enough. Now I spend my vacations in India, Thailand, or any place more chilled than here."

Like Baza, Sandra had a strong mathematical bent, and she spoke her mind with edgy humor. She often gave voice to what the rest of the team was thinking, but was afraid to say. "We're spreadsheet junkies," she would laugh, "We don't deal with reality, but what if reality comes back to bite us?"

"Well, I really admire you, Sandra," Baza stammered, unable to put the breadth of that sentiment into words. It wasn't just her discipline involving yoga but because she was smart, compulsively punctual, hardworking, and kept the group organized. She was raised a military brat whose father had been a specialist in logistics, and was also alert to business trends across the gamut of industries. On her own time, when she wasn't practicing the chair pose, downward-facing dog, or tree stand, she kept busy reading books on supply-chain management. She was also obsessed with analyzing the success of trailblazing enterprises like FedEx, Wal-Mart and Netflix, and would regularly tell Baza about the latest trend that was either emerging or peaking.

They were sitting in Starbucks and Baza was nursing the largest triple shot coffee drink he could order while Sandra sipped her Chai latte. The conversation had wandered back to work and some of Sandra's latest discoveries.

"Can you believe that Netflix delivers ninety-two percent of its orders the next day—and does it by relying on the US Postal Service for the heavy lifting? It's incredible."

"That's impressive. Was this from your light Friday night reading?" Baza asked and she laughed.

Sandra didn't exactly mother the team, but she did listen to their complaints. She also kept them supplied with café lattes with an extra shot when the pressure was on. Despite her own healthier than most lifestyle, she cheerfully accepted the vices of others. Nor did her spiritual interests seem to keep her from pursuing team productivity as the path to bigger bonuses for the entire group. She saw keeping everyone working efficiently as part of her job. Baza viewed Sandra as an island of sanity in a mostly insane sea of growing corruption. Whenever he got the chance to talk with her one on one, she was like a breath of less than polluted air. Yet he couldn't help wondering what her own personal agenda was for continuing to be part of the Moody's landscape. Was she saving up to buy an island in the Canadian wilderness where she would eventually open a health and wellness retreat?

The rest of the team was a gaggle of smart, and smart-ass young analysts who didn't hesitate to challenge Baza. They did not fully understand the opposing pressures that he was under, but questioned him because he promised that he valued their criticism, which was half-true. While day-to-day most of them went with the corporate flow—they were well-paid at Moody's and knew it—they enjoyed nothing more than picking something apart when given a chance.

It was a trait Baza harnessed in a strategic offsite location where the team was invited to poke holes in the analytical process they executed. They were also supposed to offer ideas for improving it.

Most of the loan packages were coming in from Southern California, Nevada, Arizona, and Florida—"subshine loans," the analysts called them. While most of the loans were labeled as being for primary residences, which were considered more stable and less prone to default, the analysts suspected that many of them were actually for properties purchased as vacation homes or as speculative investments.

Baza's group was constantly wrangling with Moody's investment bank clients over ratings of security offerings and the amount of equity that had to be set aside in case of default. Occasionally Big Bird or another sales executive would get involved in the mess and pretend to be mediating. But in reality, the salespeople always sided with the client; they never stood by the analytical team.

Big Bird would say, "Now Baza, you know the customer is always right," and wink.

It made Baza's stomach turn. His team called it "the switch."

Corruption was highly nuanced on Wall St. like the line between sane and crazy, the wall between right and wrong had a blur in the middle, where someone could comfortably rest for awhile.

"Why are we even here?" complained a junior analyst, nick-named "the hippie" because of her left-leaning politics and frumpy, ethnic-tinged wardrobe. She despised what she called "the bank-rupt culture of Wall Street" and lasted only two months in Baza's group before going back home to California to work in her father's real estate office. Everyone else was happy to see her go, although they did not entirely disagree with her rants. Like so many corpo-rate critics, she was overzealous, self-righteous, and never gave it a rest.

Baza often wondered who among the many strange faces at Moody's could one day be a whistleblower. He thought if it were anyone who was still hanging in, it would be Sandra.

One rainy Friday, which happened to be March 16, just 15 days before the end of the first quarter, a new pool came in to be rated at about 3:30 p.m. Tired at the end of another frantically busy week, team members groaned virtually in unison. So much for T.G.I.F. and an early night.

But no one was surprised at this latest crunch. Intent on boosting quarterly earnings and bonus payments, bankers and loan originators would work overtime to slam loan volume through the system before the quarter ended. At Moody's, a single one of these deals could generate as much as $300,000 in revenue, much of which dropped straight to the bottom line. With costs limited to computer modeling, IT expenses, and the analysts' payroll, the firm had margins any operating company would envy.

This was a Lehman Brothers deal, and the bankers were push-ing for a rating that evening. The bond wasn't due to be issued for two weeks, but the bankers couldn't wait to start selling it. If they got an early read on when the bond would be rated, the SEC would allow the banks to pre-sell. The markets were so superheated, and investors' appetites for CDOs were so huge, that the bankers knew they could have this bond fully subscribed within 24 hours of getting the green light. Everyone up and down the value chain was working overtime to make it happen and so quality controls seemed to be out the window.

Big Bird called Baza towards the end of the day. For some reason, fraternization among ratings salespeople and their firms' analytical teams had not been banned by the SEC. The implications of that oversight did not become evident until it was too late.

"Hey, *que pasa*, my little Latino pal. Got any plans for the weekend?" boomed Big Bird's familiar voice. "Why don't you come up to Lake George with us? We're taking the boat up. There'll be plenty of booze, all the food you want—our chef, too. We're just gonna kick back and relax. Why don't you join us? I'll send Mauricio over." Big Bird's driver, a sleepy-eyed immigrant from Guatemala, was used to being on call for such social gatherings.

Baza smiled, remembering the hand-rolled cigars, 60-year-old cognac, and endless wisecracking at Big Bird's last blow-out. Going to one of his big weekends was like checking into a pleasure palace.

"Unlikely. My group just got dumped on late yesterday afternoon and a couple of people have the flu. We're all gonna be working straight through until Sunday at least," Baza said, ready to pour on the guilt if he could. "But thanks. I'd love a rain check if you are offering one."

"Oh, come on. You can lean on your gang. You're the boss! Get them to hunker down and get the deal done tonight. Then you can be free tomorrow," Big Bird tried to cajole him. Baza knew that his real agenda was to get the work done before March 16, the deadline for deals that quarter, and he figured that Big Bird knew that he knew. But they both danced around it.

"Oh, now I get it. Mr. Sales wants me to pressure my people to work in high gear all night so you can appease those pricks at Lehman? Dream on," Baza said. "No way can we rate an $800 million deal in a few hours. Are you insane?" He was indignant, but also felt deflated. This was one of those moments when he regretted leaving his job in the Mayor's Office for Moody's. What had he been thinking?

"Hey, you've got it totally wrong. I'm not even involved in that deal—it's none of my business. I just thought you might like to have some fun this weekend." Big Bird eased up. We'll have a drink soon, OK? Just not tonight, I guess."

"Yup! Another time. Thanks for the offer." Baza hung up, shaking his head.

Baza's boss, Dana Fielding, also pushed him, though her approach was quite different. Pressure from her was cloaked in the language of accolades and entreaties.

"Checked on weekend volume," she said in a call on Sunday. "Your team performed spectacularly this week—amazing quality and quantity. What more could I ask? One last thing—if there's a way to finish up A-1063, that new Lehman deal, by tonight, it would help a lot."

"We will do the best we can. FYI: we got it after 3 p.m. yesterday, not a lot of time to do our job properly." Baza replied.

"I understand, Baza. But I'll hold out a prize, if you make it happen," she chuckled and hung up.

Baza's tech team were the superstars of the firm; they even reshaped the firm's long-established culture. Arguing that it was poor form to dress more formally than their tech firm clients, they won the fight for casual Friday and then turned it into casual Wednesday-through-Friday. For three days a week, they shed the white-shirt-and-red-tie uniform that had long been *de rigueur* at Goldman.

They even had their own cafeteria, of sorts, with snacks and drinks delivered all day. They wrote their own rules and created resentment throughout the firm. When the dot-com bust blew up the group, everyone else in the firm was delighted.

Baza and Fielding did not carry themselves with the same arrogance as the Goldman Sachs tech wizards had. But they were automatically set apart from the rest of the firm because they worked on the hottest and fastest-growing investment vehicle on Wall Street.

Mortgage-backed securities were not only a favored investment in the U.S., but they were also received enthusiastically by investors all around the world. The Chinese alone invested more than $500 billion in one form of MBS or another.

Banks in Europe, Saudi sheiks and financial firms in Brazil were all jumping on the MBS bandwagon—and no wonder. They were allegedly as safe as any investment on the planet, yet they offered fantastic returns. They seemed almost too good to be true.

Baza was aware of his influence at Moody's, but saw it as a cause for concern, not conceit or arrogance. Because he came to believe the team's ratings were unrealistically bullish, any sense of importance he might have had was outweighed by his sense of risk, if not impending doom.

He just remembered he was going to make that call for Trina. He was suddenly caught between the intense desire to help her get something she needed—a stable home—and a desire to protect her from this house of cards. She had been very excited about the low payments on the adjustable mortgage he had told her about, but he would have to convince her to get a 30-year fixed mortgage.

8

The week after the Lehman Brothers deal rating was done and dusted Big Bird managed to cajole Baza into coming along to the NCAA basketball playoffs in Las Vegas, which always proved to be a great opportunity for a junket with clients. He promised Baza that he would not be forced to hang out with the three Lehman bankers whose favor Big Bird wanted to curry. Big Bird and his clients were flying on the Lehman corporate jet, with Moody's picking up the rest of the tab. Baza finally agreed to come but said he was going to fly commercial.

The playoffs were guaranteed to be a wild event—the kind of gambling marathon that drew investment bankers from New York as well as venture capitalists from Silicon Valley. It was as though the Final Four had been invented for these young wealthy hotshots, while everyone else was relegated to betting on the office pool back home.

The group from Lehman considered the four-day free-for-all to be nothing more than their due. After all, they were graduates from the best schools, earned astronomical salaries and bonuses, and were lionized in the media as the glam rock stars of today. They felt they had the golden touch. The dot-com crash, just three years before, seemed like ancient history.

Baza could schmooze as necessary, but he was not in his element with these ostentatious acts of celebration and consumption as much as Big Bird, who seemed to revel in this atmosphere. Baza's sense of self derived not from aspiring to excel, but from feeling obliged to be the best. Exactly what was "best," however, was hard to say, given the tug of war between revenue-hungry corporate executives and analysts coerced into giving good ratings on too many bad deals. As he gained stature in the firm, it was a conflict Baza was encountering more frequently.

Although Baza and Big Bird had breached the wall that was supposed to separate sales and analysis more than once, neither one wanted to be blatant about it. It served no one to give the impression that Moody's was a total whore. The morning they left New York, Big Bird shared his plan with Baza.

"So here's the deal Baz, I'm going to be having dinner with the guys from Lehman around 8 tonight and I'll be coming through the lobby with them after some drinks in the bar and you need to be planning to walk through at the same time. Got it?"

"Yeah, all right," Baza said, feeling like this plan to create what seemed like a serendipitous meeting was quite ludicrous.

"Then I'll invite you to join us for dinner. They'll feel they'd been given special consideration, and then Moody's integrity will remain intact." Big Bird clapped his hands together, as if all problems were solved by this simple deception.

"You have an interesting way of defining integrity," Baza said.

True to plan, later that day Big Bird shepherded his guests past the fountains in the Bellagio's lobby and Baza appeared right on cue. "Hey, look who's here!" said Big Bird, giving a convincing impression of someone who was genuinely surprised.

"Guys, this is Baza Ponce," Big Bird said, eliciting a round of handshaking. "What are you doing here in Sin City, Baza? Are you attending some boring housing conference? You guys know Baza, don't you? He runs our MBS review team; they spit out more AAA bonds than any other firm on the Street. He's a big believer in what you guys are doing."

Baza squirmed, and quickly cut Big Bird off before he spewed out any more embarrassing chatter.

"No, no boring conference this time. I just decided to make a detour on my way back from L.A. I'm rooting for Dartmouth to make the NCAA pairings," Baza said.

"Dartmouth? Dream on, my friend, not a chance," Big Bird said. "Want to join us for dinner and lick your wounds after hearing Dartmouth didn't make the cut? Meet us at the steakhouse downstairs for dinner. I'll add you to the reservation."

Baza murmured his agreement, then went off to find a craps table. As always, he was operating on two distinct levels. There was the group experience, where he acted as a team player. Then there was the solo journey—a night of gambling, drinking and hookers. In the morning he would once again be alone, regretting it all.

He could lose himself at the craps table. There was something about happy people rolling the dice that exhilarated him. It was about optimism, good times...the shared experience that happened when the dice were hot. Then a reckless mood took over, as if the people around the table were a small band of rebels seizing the casino and taking no prisoners.

In a place like this, Baza could tap into the ambient electricity, but still remain aloof. His pattern was to drift from table to table, hunting for hot dice and stray women. Las Vegas was full of them: Women who were cutting loose and women who were drunk. Ladies of the night, and women who were looking for nothing more than a one-night stand.

No one came to Vegas in search of a serious relationship, which made the rules of the game much simpler. No entanglements, no complications, and only minimal risks. Though that wasn't always the case.

A junior Wall Street trader once attended a bachelor party for the head of his desk at one of the best Vegas hotels. At the wedding, he drank copious amounts of Cristal, then moved on to cognac, and finally to Scotch. Around 1 in the morning, he picked up a hooker at the MGM Grand and took her back to his room.

After sex, he went into the bathroom and came out to find the young woman rifling through his wallet. He went berserk, put his hands around her throat, and squeezed until she stopped moving. His way of dealing with the situation was to drag the young woman's nude body out into the hallway and try to flush the contents of her purse down the toilet. Tried and convicted of first-degree murder, he's sitting in a Nevada penitentiary with another 22 years to serve. His trip ended up being something other than the party-hearty, three-day bender he'd had in mind.

Baza played blackjack for about 20 minutes, never landing at a hot table. As soon as he had a string of bets on the table, putting him "on the verge of greatness," as he called it, the roller would hit a seven and wipe him out.

He retreated to the lobby bar at the Wynn, a circular space that was defined by a huge round canopy, making it feel open, yet intimate at the same time. He found a seat and struck up a conversation with three women from Fox Entertainment in L.A.; they were warming up for a company off-site starting the next day.

"We listen to the bobbleheads in the morning, then go shopping or to the spa while the golfers hit the ball around. In the evening, we get dressed up, have cocktails, and then dinner at one of the top restaurants. It beats the pants off three days in the office, wouldn't you say?" laughed Brenda, a husky 40-something with tinted blond hair and acne scars. The women hooted loudly as they traded off-color jokes. Baza wondered how different these women's personalities were from when they were back home. He had seen on multiple occasions how Vegas seemed to transform people, lowering inhibitions past the point of no return, the heady combination of booze, gambling and excess transforming the shyest of wallflowers into cascading vines of bougainvillea.

Bored with the giggling trio, Baza began to think about what Las Vegas, New York, and Los Angeles had in common. They were all places of excess where value and cost did not match up; the math was off. In these high-cost markets, it was all too easy for people to go on a consumption binge they financed by using their homes as bank accounts, abetted by the "convenience checks" that came with their credit lines. Baza thought of his father, who would say the banks should give people an old-fashioned savings pass-book with their credit lines, not a wad of blank checks.

Companies, too, were on a spending spree. Many major firms such as Moody's spent hundreds of thousands—sometimes even millions of dollars—on off-site meetings, retreats, conferences, holiday parties and banquets. These amounts were just a tiny fraction of the billions in revenue that the firms generated.

After a few more laughs with the L.A. ladies, he went back to his room, cleaned up and came down for dinner. Before meeting up with the others, he knocked back a Maker's Mark and tried his hand at blackjack. There was no joy at the tables and Dartmouth did not make the cut to be among the 64 teams in the NCAA playoffs. There was far more misery in this town than victory, yet people kept coming back.

At dinner, Big Bird sandwiched Baza in between Matt Borero from Lehman and a special guest, Linda O'Dell, a senior vice president at Jetsco Mortgage, one of the largest subprime lenders in the country. The circle was complete: the company that made the loans, the company that bought the loans, then sold them to investors, and the company that rated the packaged loans.

Baza buttonholed O'Dell, getting her read on the market. That also gave him an excuse to brush off the Lehman guys, since anything other than purely social conversation with them would be crossing the line.

"So where are you from, Linda?"

"Originally, San Diego. I moved to New York a few years ago with my husband and switched from selling real estate to mortgages," Linda said, downing her third Scotch in 30 minutes.

Baza noticed she put herself in charge of ordering wine, which she proceeded to do with abandon in terms of both price and volume. The drunker she got, the giddier she became, and the more outspoken about the mortgage market.

"We are printing money; it's beyond ridiculous," she said, swishing her wine glass in the air for added emphasis. "Production volume is through the roof, and if you can brush your teeth, we can get you a home loan."

Baza nodded benignly, not wanting to give any impression of necessarily agreeing with or contradicting her. She carried on, unfazed.

"A bubble? What do you think? Of course it's a bubble! So, get it while you can. You heard it here."

Then, like a good 50 percent of all drunks, based on Baza's observations, she turned crude and took aim at the men at the table. "You guys created this," she said, pointing a wavering finger at the Lehman contingent. "You're the ones to blame if it all blows up…'cuz I know that as long as Baza's gang says my shit is clean, you'll keep buying it."

There was an awkward moment, but the tension dissipated as the food arrived and she shifted her indignation to the waiter, complaining her steak was too rare. She had eaten almost an entire loaf of bread while soaking up the booze, so it was hard to imagine she had room for anything else. Later Big Bird explained that he had no choice but to invite her because she was in town and did a huge business with Lehman.

Deciding that the risk of professional compromise was less painful than humiliation at the hands of a drunken subprime mortgage lender, Baza spent the rest of the evening chatting with Phil Stein, an intense-looking Lehman VP who bundled loans. No matter what direction you tried to steer a conversation towards with these guys, Baza thought, they kept reverting to shop talk.

"We have been getting help from the guys over at Standard and Poor's figuring out the pricing on these instruments, and we told Michael we would love to spend some time with your team," said Stein, picking the raspberries off his mascarpone napoleon. "The better we understand your analytics, the better we'll be at making packaging decisions. Are you open to that?" he asked.

Baza was polite but gave a non-answer. "We help where we can, and where we can't we don't," he smiled. "Check with Michael, happy to do what I can."

When the group began to order after-dinner drinks, Baza left, with the excuse that he had to get up early for his morning flight back to New York. At this point, O'Dell was promising to "show you guys my new tattoo."

Luckily, Big Bird and his entourage were staying at the Wynn. Baza was at the Bellagio, so he could still find trouble on his own.

Trouble would have to wait, though. He had a voicemail from Trina, who he hadn't heard from in the past week. As it turned out, she hadn't responded to his messages because she'd been visiting relatives in the Philippines, but now she was also in Vegas for the porn industry's biggest trade show, which attracted more than 100,000 movie producers, magazine publishers, and sex toy peddlers. She said she was in a contest for "Best Tranny Legs" being sponsored by Tranny Magazine at the Paris Hotel.

Baza called right back, adopting the teasing, playful tone they shared with each other. "You got through customs? They'll let anyone come into this country." He recalled a story she had told him about coming back from Paris, and what happened when the customs officer examining her passport saw that it identified her as a male.

"Don't be confused," had been Trina's confident reply. She may have been a member of a repressed fringe minority, but she did not live her life that way. She was simply who she was, with no cowering, no defensiveness and no ugly reactions.

"Pardon me?" said the customs officer. "It says here you are a male."

"You know what I am, but you can do a strip search to make sure if you would like," she offered.

He stamped her passport.

Trina came over to meet Baza at the Bellagio. They talked, she did a nylon show and they went downstairs to gamble. As they cruised the tables, Baza looked around and leaned over to whisper in Trina's ear, "You know what? You're the best-looking woman in the casino, and you certainly have the best legs."

Their relationship had always been casual, no strings attached, no questions asked. But when he said goodbye to her this time, even though they were both headed back to New York on separate flights, he found himself wanting to know when he was going to see her again, yet he managed to keep himself from asking.

9

Baza was only back in New York a few days before he had to make a work trip to London. On the flight across the pond to have meetings with Lehman's U.K. office, Baza pored over the latest batch of housing market reports with an escalating feeling of dread. Home prices in the Silicon Valley neighborhood where he'd lived had jumped another 23 percent, and it was the same story in upscale suburbs and vacation spots all across the country. How much longer could this go on?

At breakfast in his London hotel the next morning, Baza unfurled the morning paper and nearly choked on his poached egg when he read an article, buried on an inside page, quoting testimony given that week by Frank Partnoy, professor at the University of San Diego School of Law, before the United States Senate Committee on Banking, Housing, and Urban Affairs.

"The evidence against credit rating agencies is damning. The problems I raised in 2002 have grown exponentially, and the dangers presented by the rating agency system are also much greater," Partnoy had told the committee.

"At the same time, Moody's and Standard and Poor's are more profitable and powerful than ever. Moody's shares have risen in value to a total market capitalization of about $20 billion, more than either General Motors or Bear Stearns. In fact, Moody's shares have increased in value by more than five hundred percent since they were issued, during a period when the rest of the market was down."

Baza knew his team was giving triple-A ratings to mortgage pools full of loans just like the one described in the ad. It was a massive confidence game that kept escalating. The solid ratings reassured investors all was well, which created more demand for mortgage-backed securities, which put more pressure on lenders and mortgage brokers to make high-risk loans — the riskier the mortgages, the greater the danger of a wholesale collapse. The house of cards was teetering, that's for sure.

Baza's last meeting that day was at 2 p.m. with a Lehman analyst, Rick Bunting, who was of similar mind and had become a good friend. They had known some of the same people from back in the Silicon Valley days but had somehow never directly crossed paths back then. On Bunting's last trip to the U.S., they had partied together in the Hamptons, drank too much, and gotten into a heated debate over how much culpability they would have in a coming mortgage meltdown. But they were both asking the same questions about what would happen and when.

Since then Bunting had become even more vocal about his concerns. Their meeting quickly moved from fine points of bond analysis to the bigger issues on both their minds.

"You know what's going on, Baza, you can't just ignore it," Bunting said, pounding his desk emphatically. "You read *The Economist*—hell, man, you were quoted in it! That's not some lame blogger; that's the leading conservative financial magazine of the world calling it a bubble. You've become an expert on all this, but let's face it: You're carrying the industry's water. You're the one telling people they don't have to worry. The truth is, you've got a big hand in this mess, my friend."

"I hear you, Rick, I hear you. I just...don't know what to do. Or what I can do," Baza said, his palms turned upward, feeling like he was giving a paltry excuse for his role in the growing mess.

At that moment, Baza flashed back to Honduras and the case of a prominent rancher his parents had known. The handsome scion of an illustrious and wealthy family, the man had taken up with a woman far below his class. When the affair came to light, he left both his girlfriend and his wife and family and disappeared altogether. "He got in his car, headed in one direction or another, and was never heard from again," Baza's father would say. He had recited the story many times, intending it as an object lesson. "If only his shame had not driven him away from the truth."

When Baza first heard the story, he was 17 and had just broken up with his girlfriend. He understood that coping was easier for some than others. "Being strong is overrated," he had thought.

Baza took Bunting's warnings seriously. He was a hard charger driven by keen intelligence, competitiveness and a strong sense of propriety. A lanky six-feet-five, Bunting was obsessed with bicycling. He had traveled all over the British Isles by bike and would ship his Bianchi ahead of any business trip that allowed the opportunity for an extended ride. His bike was as important to him as any personal relationship.

Bunting also knew the U.S. market. Raised in California, he had earned his MBA at Stanford, worked in San Francisco for a time, and then fled to London with his girlfriend after the dot-com bust. He quickly became the star analyst at Lehman, which was then putting its best and brightest on the Mortgage-backed Securities Desk. Bunting helped the desk generate record profits, but he was also known for being truthful and philosophical about the firm's exploits, whether others liked hearing it or not.

In private, Bunting would put all diplomacy aside and drift into a Kafkaesque frame of mind. "What is this all about?" he would say, shaking his head ruefully. "I feel like my life is some dreadful movie, and I am sitting watching myself with disgust. Why are we mixed up in this nonsense? Just so Americans can buy more stuff? It's insane."

Bunting's mental and philosophical rigor had been forged in the chaos of his childhood. The son of hippie parents who spent years living in communes, he had once watched his mother fall into a fit of insanity while on a mescaline trip. "I love order, math, and the good life because I despised the mayhem around my family," he once told Baza.

Nevertheless, Bunting's father had always been one to insist on total honesty in all dealings. One episode that always stayed with him happened when Bunting was five or six years old and out walking with his father. He found a dollar bill in the weeds along a fence and picked it up. His father would not let him pocket the dollar, and instead made him walk up the lane to the door of the nearest house and return the money, warning that he should not accept it even if it was offered.

Bunting was like the voice of Baza's conscience—so much so that a heated exchange with him could drive Baza right into one of his panic attacks. Bunting knew exactly which buttons to push.

"Someone has got to be a whistleblower. Maybe it's you?" Bunting looked at him expectantly, waiting for an answer, which Baza didn't give.

Yet he knew Bunting was right. Where were the Buntings back in New York, he wondered.

As if one gut-wrenching session with Bunting weren't enough, before leaving his colleague's London office, Baza asked whether they might have dinner together. In the back of his mind he hoped that one more push from Bunting might give him the courage to go back to New York and take dramatic action.

Surprisingly calm and collected after his rant, Bunting was game. "Works for me. Are you staying at Blakes? Maybe we'll see a movie star." Blakes was a boutique hotel and restaurant on Roland Gardens in upscale South Kensington. They agreed to meet at the hotel at 8 p.m..

After leaving Bunting's office, Baza was in a state. His throat was dry and his heart was pounding—a full-blown panic attack in the making. He knew he was complicit in what could easily become a collapse of the global financing system. *Oh my God, what have I done* thought Baza, drenched in perspiration from the anxiety of it all.

He knew how to treat panic attacks. Ample doses of adventure, booze, gambling and women offered the best temporary relief.

Crazed after his meeting with Bunting, he plotted his afternoon and early evening: a long walk, one or two beers at a pub, a couple of cigarettes, a martini and then a red wine or two at a nice hotel like the Rivoli Bar at the Ritz.

He would then be appropriately fortified to enter a trouble zone—Piccadilly Circus, where every flavor of sexual encounter was for sale or displayed as window shopping.

That would leave just enough time for a cab back to his hotel and a hot shower before meeting Bunting for dinner. It would appear that he'd retired to his room for a long hot bath and a chapter or two of his favorite book. His real activities, of course, would give him another set of things to fret about.

Before leaving Bunting's office, Baza had slipped a hint about possibly canceling the dinner. "I'm feeling a slight tickle...I hope it's nothing coming on. If I feel worse, I'll call you and ask for a rain check," Baza said, clearing his throat conspicuously. He always liked to leave himself an out, just in case something more promising popped up. It heightened his sense of danger and allowed for the possibility of having more fun than rehashing scenarios of doom with Bunting.

"Understood," said Bunting, who had seen this act before.

After a pint at a pub around from Bunting's office, he walked into the Rivoli in the Ritz with its visual feast of art deco-style camphor wood, satinwood, alabaster, gold leaf and Lalique glass. The Rivoli was the best prospect for finding a dangerous older woman, an attractive gold digger to whom he could promise the sun and moon. He could deal with the backwash in the days and weeks ahead, if he was so careless as to give her his true contact information or, worse still, his business card.

If things went his way, within hours he would be promising trips, gifts and devotion to some complete stranger. He would lose control.

When that happened, things could get dicey. Take that time in Hartford two years ago. He was sitting alone at a table for two in a downtown hotel bar. Gloria Burke, forty-something and dressed as though she were auditioning for *The Paris Hilton Story*, came up to him and asked if the seat next to him was available. He took a big swallow of his drink and responded, "for the rest of your life."

The consequences of that line took a year to untangle, during which the woman—whose brother, she informed him, was a well-known trial lawyer—would repeatedly recall the line and insist it represented some sort of contract. One day, she called his cell phone 53 times and left at least 30 messages, which grew more and more threatening as the day dragged on.

Baza dismissed the episode with a favorite line from one of his friends: "Men are stupid and women are crazy."

His London escapade was following his familiar routine: a solo journey and an adventure that would haunt him later. He might forget pieces of the experience, but the risks of the adventure and whatever trouble he encountered were indelibly fixed in his brain. He was a deliberate sinner, one who never questioned the morality of his actions going in, but wallowed in shame ever after. Even then, he rarely thought about the reasons for his actions. He was focused solely on his fear of what might happen if he was found out. Public humiliation. Or worse, his family discovering what he really was.

Baza's father had often said, "You can do whatever you want if you are willing to face the consequences."

The Honduran liked the idea of being an optimist, but knew he fell into the camp of being more of an eternal pessimist. He held onto negative incidents from his past like women safeguarded their good jewelry. If he had one hundred positive or uplifting experiences, but had one bad thing happen to him, he would forever ponder the mistake, imagining all the ways it might get him into trouble. It was a scenario he played in his mind over and over again—the mistake from his past that would always catch up with him.

His most elaborate mind tales were multi-layered. He would think of a misdeed from his past and then connect it with a current news event. Almost anything might set him off. Reading *The Wall Street Journal*, for instance, could trigger a panic attack if he connected key words in the story with a past cause of shame. The *Journal* had recently run a story about Craigslist settling with 40 state attorney generals over prostitutes advertising on the popular online classified site. Baza could not bring himself to read the entire story because he became convinced that his trolling of Craigslist's personals might find its way into some database that the government could monitor.

His panic grew as his imagination began to spin out of control. Like all Moody's employees, he had been fingerprinted and his background filed with government overseers. Had he ever trolled the personals from his office? Of course he had, foolishly, with a corporate IP address attached to his name. He would often lock the glass door to his office, close the blinds he had installed for privacy, and masturbate as he surfed porn sites. It was the extreme inappropriateness and the danger of the situation that raised his excitement to a fever pitch.

Over and over again, he returned to his favorite sites, like EroticMoments.com, which blatantly featured women peddling prostitution and had a transsexual section showing plenty of the nylon-clad legs he loved.

Baza's anxious imaginings got even wilder after New York Governor Eliot Spitzer was busted for wiring bank funds to what proved to be a front for a high-end prostitution ring. Baza became obsessed with the idea that the government would somehow connect his questionable mortgage analyses at Moody's with his clandestine adventures. Experiencing a sense of impending doom, he pictured a massive white-collar indictment with video of his shame running over and over on CNN, Fox News, and all the rest.

He could see it now: Headlines screaming "Corrupt Mortgage Analyst Snared in Transsexual Scandals." He would be caught with a transgender hooker, blamed for financial disaster in the subprime mortgage market, or both.

Baza now craved the combination he always sought to soothe and distract himself when panicked—that is, plenty of alcohol plus an intimate connection with an intriguing stranger. But on this day, the Rivoli Bar offered little promise of the latter. Baza settled for the alcohol and a long conversation with the bartender about the U.K. housing market. When the bartender, Ed, learned that Baza worked in mortgages on Wall Street, he was eager to share his retirement plan with him.

"I actually just bought a flat outside of London, which I'm confident will rise in value at least 20 or 30 percent in the next two years. I plan to cash in on my home equity 10 to 15 years from now, to supplement my pension, or before then if I get made redundant."

"But how are you certain it will increase in value?" asked Baza. "What goes up must come down, right? That's how markets work. Aren't you worried that things might not go the way you expect?" He was unable to keep himself from projecting his earlier business conversation onto this hard-working man who was merely excited about his house purchase.

"Listen mate, the housing market in London just goes up, it doesn't know another direction. It's bloody mad, but true," the bartender sounded irritated with Baza for raining on his parade.

It was almost as though Baza was trying to find someone else to blame for the woes he had helped to create—it was the borrower, the stupid weak borrower who refused to see the risks of the housing market or of the loans they were taking out. It was their fault...not Moody's, not Wall Street's. It wasn't because of greed, but because of the bums who were ignorant enough to get a home loan in the first place. If they had been more responsible, then lenders would not have originated the loans, Wall Street would not have bought them, and he would not have had to rate them.

His attitude upset Ed, who began banging bottles and clanking glasses.

"No, I don't waste a moment worrying about prices going up or down. That's a job for blokes like you, who work in financial markets."

"As a matter of fact, yes. I'm just saying what goes up, has to come down at some point. Doesn't seem like a bulletproof retirement plan."

You blokes take all manner of risks and don't lose any sleep at night. I'm just a bartender. I work hard, go home and pay my mortgage."

"It was just a suggestion."

"I count on guys like you to figure this stuff out for the rest of us." Ed turned his attention to a grizzled older man in a cowboy hat. "Who's this, John Wayne? What can I get you, sir?"

Baza suddenly felt ashamed for his boorish behavior. Taking on a bartender was stupid. Clearly, he was out of sorts. Blame is the first line of defense against responsibility; he learned that a long time ago.

He was also guilty of carrying two conflicting thoughts in his head, instead of landing on one and making a decision. It's what George Orwell, in his book 1984 described as "doublethink."

The power of holding two contradictory beliefs in one's mind simultaneously, and accepting both of them. To tell deliberate lies while genuinely believing in them, to forget any fact that has become inconvenient, and then, when it becomes necessary again, to draw it back from oblivion for just so long as it is needed, to deny the existence of objective reality and all the while to take account of the reality which one denies— all this is indispensably necessary. Even in using the word doublethink it is necessary to exercise doublethink. For by using the word one admits that one is tampering with reality; by a fresh act of doublethink one erases this knowledge; and so on indefinitely, with the lie always one leap ahead of the truth.

The conversation with Ed was over. They both had jumped the Ritz protocol wall and had to scramble back to where they each belonged. The difference was that customers are allowed such rudeness; the help is not.

Baza had somehow slipped into that American classless mode he found so puzzling when he first came to America—that hyper-democratic paradigm where classes mingle and everyone is friendly and chatty, as though they were economic, social, and political equals. Even though they clearly were not.

In Honduras, class still thrived; the roles were clear and the benefits even more so. If he went into a drug store and there was a line, the clerk would make eye contact with Baza, wave him ahead and wait on him first.

"Another bourbon, Knob Creek? Goes down warm, doesn't it? Need anything else? How about some chips or nuts?" Ed was back, having decided it behooved him to be solicitous to his customer. Baza's attention snapped back to the bar; until Ed spoke, he had been drifting, not even there. Now all was back to normal: the bar servant humbles himself to the well-heeled visitor and everyone smiles. Baza was certain to leave a big tip, helping the bartender to afford his fat mortgage. This is how it works.

That morning, in the *Financial Times*, Baza read an article on how to moderate your drinking. One tip was to limit consumption to one drink every 60 minutes.

Baza glanced at his watch. He had been sitting at the bar for just over half an hour. So far, he had slung down two double bourbons—four shots of liquor. That meant he was drinking at a pace of 15 minutes per cocktail.

Oh well.

Baza had several reasons to fret about his propensity for drinking. His older brother had died in a car crash in Monaco, drunk out of his mind. Baza's first drink was never his last, which meant he had a control problem. And it was abundantly clear that alcohol impaired his judgment. He secretly struggled with alcohol, always testing some new system of abstinence or moderation. His current strategy was moderation: have some fun but stop short of going to the dark side.

For a few days he kept track of his consumption, alternating his alcoholic drinks with diet coke, mineral water, lemonade or coffee. He was careful not to drink on an empty stomach and waited until an hour had passed before ordering his next drink.

His other rules were generally impossible: Try not to attend parties where alcohol is served; don't drink when sad or depressed; don't use booze to alleviate stress or escape problems. Complying with those strictures was hopeless. Alcohol was often the only relief he had. He thought about Sandra and how she had switched her vice to yoga. He wasn't sure he had the DNA for such healthy discipline.

He got up from the stool, took his drink and walked to an out-door table under an awning outside. The late afternoon chill felt good. He pulled out a pack of Dunhill Lights and lit one up.

With a single drag on the cigarette, he exposed his lungs to 43 cancer-causing chemicals. But the tobacco also lit up his senses and helped him manage the screeching opera of doom and joy that continually played in his head. That first hit of nicotine, going right to the brain, was enough to unleash the swirl of feelings that both aggravated his paranoia and gave him blissful relief.

In an odd way, smoking also gave him a license to get in trou-ble. Once sullied by the habit, he could get down into the dirt and rub it all over himself.

The booze, the cigarettes and the minor clash with the bar-tender prompted a whiff of Latin anger and machismo. *Fuck it—never mind what anyone else says. You're fine, they're stupid.*

He could feel his facial expression, knew what it looked like, as though he were watching a video of himself. A stiff jaw, a clenched, sneering smile—it was an ugly, arrogant loathsome look. He was caught in a quixotic pattern of loving and hating himself all day long, a clash that shattered any peace or calm he ever hoped to achieve. Serenity was always out of reach.

Intoxicated enough to go anywhere and try anything, he jumped in a cab and headed for Piccadilly Circus.

10

Relieved to be back in New York, Baza met Big Bird in the bar of the Ritz-Carlton on Central Park South. It was one of Big Bird's favorite haunts, mainly because he enjoyed telling his woes to Norman, who was one of the most famous bartenders in the world. Your classic nice Jewish boy from the Bronx, Norman was as devoted to the Yankees as he was to taking care of his best customers.

While fending off any predators or blatant gold-diggers who found their way to the Ritz, he also reveled in the exploits of male customers who brought in their mistresses or found new conquests at the bar. Norman was known for expertly coaching his customers on how to manage their indiscretions discreetly. "There is a right way to do wrong," he would tell them; it was one of his best-known lines.

"Hello, my little Latino friend," exclaimed Big Bird, who always greeted Baza the same way. "How does it feel to be standing in front of the biggest hotshot on Wall Street, the king of MBS, the prince of the American Dream, the hero of millions of peasant homeowners. Here I am, your one and only asshole friend." Even more ebullient than usual, Big Bird wrapped his portly Irish frame around Baza and lifted him a good eight inches off the ground.

Baza guessed that Big Bird outweighed him by one hundred pounds or more. Not only did he have a prodigious appetite for food and drink, but he also ate at top speed, demolishing huge meals just as rapidly as he talked. Like Mike Tyson, Big Bird needed a high caloric intake because he burned so much in his relentless drive to get ahead.

"I need you to do me a favor, Baza. Come with me to Goldman Sachs tomorrow and help me explain the structure on one of their big deals," Big Bird said as he avoided meeting Baza's eyes. "They need the process explained by a smart guy like you so they can get the rating they feel their package deserves."

"Yeah, right, Goldman Sachs needs me," muttered Baza, who was always uncomfortable with the idea of helping one of Big Bird's clients structure a deal. "Is it really kosher for the head of MBS analytics to be telling Goldman what they have to do to get a better rating?" he asked, knowing full well that it was not.

"It's not like I'm asking you to cook the numbers or anything," Big Bird hedged. "All we're doing is helping them understand how things work."

As the firm's profits rose to spectacular heights, a mood of "anything goes" seemed to be taking hold. Baza's team was feeling growing pressure from the sales side of the shop. They were being invited more and more frequently to discuss deal structures and fees with clients.

Both Baza and Fielding let this happen by degrees without really thinking about what they were doing. They fended off such interactions with clients for a while, but had been worn down by the nonstop boosterism of Big Bird and other executive types. Even though Baza's team was overworked, they received a steady stream of company reports and memos exhorting them to meet revenue targets, best the competition and attract more deal flow.

Market share was becoming more important than market risk. The water cooler chatter was more about company expansion, opportunity, promotions, year-end bonuses and the bullish mood all across the country.

Over the past two weeks, Baza had started receiving instructions from Dana Fielding to spend more and more time interacting directly with bankers, helping them structure their deals. He was invited to call them by their first names and given glimpses into their personal lives. Client relationships had become decidedly cozy, all of which had started to make Baza very uneasy.

So much for the wall between church and state. It had been breached so many times that it existed only in theory.

At the same time, Baza and his people operated with virtually no controls over how rating decisions were ultimately made. The team was given some license to override the statistical models and often did. Rarely did it depart from the models in order to downgrade a loan package. It was almost always an upgrade designed to please sales and marketing.

Any discussion of revising the models revolved not around the idea of allowing for a drop in home prices, but around ways they could give high ratings to more deals.

On the one hand, Baza's people, especially the outspoken Melissa Glover and Sandra Cherovich, were openly cynical about the quality of the loan packages and the speed with which they were expected to rate them. But they were also euphoric at the contribution they could make to the company's growth. As the raises and bonuses kept escalating, they went from being cynics to being enthusiastic fans.

The longer a bubble keeps going, and the bigger it gets, the stupider the skeptics feel. Many make the shift from critic to cheerleader. In fact, skeptics often end up being the most ardent cheerleaders of all, as though seeking forgiveness for their lack of belief. In this kind of atmosphere, greed overrides all other impulses and becomes good.

Baza saw what was going on, but had no idea how to stop it. Having crossed the line, he was now in this thing up to his eyeballs, and knew he was putting both himself and his team in peril.

Baza needed to hear a voice of sanity in the madhouse and sought out Roger Jordoin whose office was a couple of floors above his. Jordoin's job, as the firm's Vice President of Credit Analysis, was to look for trouble. He trailed the analyses done by Baza's group, seeking to ferret out any problems with loan packages after the bonds had been sold. If his group found problems, the bonds could be re-priced, throwing everything into a tizzy, not something that had happened very often with subprime loan pools.

He flopped into the well-worn leather chair in Jordoin's office.

"Baza, good to see you! To what do I owe this unexpected visit?" Jordoin kept typing away on his laptop, yet he always seemed glad to see Baza.

"I just don't know, Roger, I just don't know how much longer..." Baza trailed off, shaking his head.

"I'm well aware of the pressure that Mayberry had put on the analytics team." Jordoin paused from his typing and leveled his gaze at Baza. "However, you do realize the company could be in serious jeopardy if your team succumbs to the demands of the sales group. If it comes to light that the bond ratings process is tainted, the public outcry and investigation could do to Moody's what the Enron blow-up did to Arthur Andersen, and we all know how that party ended."

At Moody's, Jordoin was the enforcer—the one responsible for maintaining the integrity of the wall between sales and analytics— although Baza felt he was too weak for the job. Still, he perceived that Jordoin was highly ambitious, although he didn't look it. At five-feet-six with a pudgy face, oversized aviator glasses, and a stumpy body, he had the meek, pasty-faced look of an accountant, and the wardrobe to match.

"I'm well aware. But it's like trying to save the Titanic after it's already hit the iceberg. And that is between you and me." Baza said.

"Yes, I just noticed this morning that mortgage default rates are creeping up and home prices aren't wildly increasing any longer; in fact they're even declining in some markets." Jordoin said. "I hear that Mayberry has been working on a scheme to develop a new product that Moody's can market through a subsidiary joint venture. The idea may have been a good one on its face, but in this volatile, fishbowl environment, I worry it's going to give all the wrong signals to clients and especially to regulators."

"Maybe you can have a quiet word with him?" Baza asked, and they both chuckled. It was hard to imagine anyone having a quiet word with Big Bird.

"Yeah right. We both know Michael is a rainmaker. The clients he brings in account for more than a third of Moody's revenues. At the same time, if the firm is guilty of crossing any ethical lines, Michael is probably involved. I told my deputy, Marsha Coyle, just last week that he's going to bring this firm down if we don't put a lid on him, just like Jeff Skilling wrecked Enron."

"Well, good luck with that. I don't envy your position, Roger," Baza stood up to head back to his office.

"Thanks. Um...actually, sit back down if you don't mind. Michael's on his way over here and I have a feeling I may need a witness to our conversation."

"What do you mean?" Baza was alarmed and didn't want to give Big Bird the impression that he had been chatting about him with Jordoin.

"Don't worry, it's all on me. This doesn't implicate you in any way. I just sent him an email a few minutes ago to let him know that he's been called to a meeting with the auditors. He should be just about here by now." Sure enough, Jordoin looked towards the door as he heard Big Bird's voice booming down the hallway ahead of him.

"Jordoin, I hope your ass is in your chair!"

He strode in, red-faced, and angrily shoved aside the red leather chair, Jordoin gestured for him to take. Big Bird ignored Baza and leaned across Jordoin's large oak desk with his fingers splayed out wide, knocking over a family picture and a bobble-head figure of Derek Jeter.

"Do you know the story of the brass ball and the glass ball, you asshole?" he shouted, the veins bulging in his neck. "No, wait... let me re-phrase that. Do you know the story of the brass ball and glass ball, you miserable little twat?"

Big Bird reached into his pockets and whipped out two identically-sized spheres. With his left hand, he slammed the brass ball down on the desk so hard that a chip of veneer flew into the air and Jordoin almost tipped over backward in his chair. Baza winced and desperately wished he had left minutes earlier. Big Bird cradled the glass ball with his right hand and slowly set it down on the desk with exaggerated care.

He leaned even closer to Jordoin, looking ready to climb onto the desk as he whispered hoarsely, "This brass ball is Moody's. We can drop it forty floors down the elevator shaft and it will be just fine. This glass ball is SB-111. If we drop it one inch, it will shatter."

Big Bird drew himself up to his full height, screaming "Do NOT fuck with my glass ball again! Do you hear me? DO NOT FUCK WITH MY GLASS BALL, you butt-licking pussy!"

His anger was so intense that his face was now nearly purple as he spluttered profanities at Jordoin.

SB-111 was a proposed joint venture with Fair Isaac, the firm behind the FICO credit score, the Mortgage Bankers Association, and the National Association of Realtors. The plan was to create a new home price-tracking index that would enable the trading of housing futures. In essence, it would let investors bet on the future direction of the housing market; it would also be another indicator of investors' confidence in the asset class.

It was a bold venture – one that would move Moody's directly into the commodity trading business. Big Bird planned to partner with all of the major investment banks, which would operate as his sales channel for securities based on the index. But rather than licensing the index to the banks, he proposed that Moody's get a percentage of each investment transaction.

"Nobody else has the *cojones* to come up with something like this," Big Bird bragged. "It takes courage and vision to invent new products."

SB-111 would mean a radical shift in Moody's business strategy, one almost as audacious as its move, back in the 1970s, from an independent subscription model to one in which the investment banks paid Moody's to rate their securities.

The firm's executives weren't sure what to think. They loved the revenue projections that Big Bird was putting forward with his concept, but they were hesitant to get into a business that would so obviously compromise their standing as an independent rating service. The investment banks were sure to salivate over it, but what would the regulators say?

Jordoin's own sense of self-preservation seemed to kick in and he tried to smooth things over. "Listen, Mayberry, I'm not making you out to be the bad guy. Everybody knows you're the mainstay of our business. Besides, aren't you from southern Illinois? Land of Lincoln, strong Midwestern values, right?" said Jordoin quickly. "It's just that I have to make sure our asses are covered here—you know that. Otherwise this thing will get shot down before it even gets off the ground."

"Yeah, well, as long as we all remember we're on the same team," said a suddenly subdued Big Bird, whose fury seemed to have blown itself out in his tirade. He picked up the balls from the desk and pocketed them, pulled up the chair he'd shoved aside earlier, and slumped down in it heavily. Temporarily worn out, he turned philosophical with Jordoin, seeming to curry his favor but also wanting an audience for his own concerns.

"Baza here is worried the housing market is turning. Right, my man?" he looked over at Baza, as if noticing him in the room for the first time. "What do you think? If you agree, we had better make some quick moves. We can't just rate these things AAA one day and BBB the next. We'll look like fools and the market will collapse," frowned Big Bird, knowing that this was the wrong guy with whom to share his concerns.

"I know you're just doing your job. And you know what, you and me, we're not really so different at the end of the day, are we? We work for the same company, we both live with our families in Connecticut, we commute on the same train to work, and we shit sitting down. And who knows, maybe we even screw some of the same women," Big Bird laughed while Jordoin winced.

That was one of the problems with Wall Street, thought Baza, wishing for a large Scotch. It was not just a business sector, but also a subculture—one populated by tens of thousands of smart, relentlessly driven people, all of them with more or less the same sorts of backgrounds, same values, same objectives. And, more to the point, the same way of thinking.

While groupthink helps to grease decision-making, it is dangerous during times of speculative frenzy, because it creates an atmosphere in which all those who aren't cheerleaders are ignored or shunned.

"Don't worry, we're looking into it. I am setting up meetings with the executive team to kick around some scenarios. Now let's relax...go have a drink. We've all had enough stress this week," Jordoin said in a placating tone.

The possibility of failure was not something Big Bird thought about much. He was always one to concentrate on the opportunities. But something about the way things were shaping up was making him uneasy. His customary optimism was missing.

Big Bird shot a glance across the desk at Jordoin. "Yes, a drink..." he said, looking oddly dazed. "Anyone join me?"

"I'm in," Baza said, eager for an excuse to dip out of the office for a while. "Roger, join us?"

"You guys go on; I've got a bit more work to do." Jordoin said, waving them off, as if Big Bird's outburst had never happened.

11

Two days later, Baza had to attend a conference in Chicago and found himself leaving from Trina's studio and heading straight to the airport. He was extremely comfortable in her company, which created a mixture of heady pleasure in Baza, combined with the usual dose of anxiety. He knew he needed to be careful and not grow too comfortable or too fond of her, as he couldn't help feeling that was just bound not to go well. But that morning she had insisted on waking up at the same time as him and making him a traditional Filipino breakfast of Silog, which was a mixture of fried garlic rice, egg, tomatoes, and pickled unripe papaya.

It was a little much for Baza's stomach at that early hour, but he was so touched by the gesture that he couldn't help but try to eat it. Luckily, she made good coffee, so that helped him get it down as she sat across from him, watching him eat, with a proud, self-satisfied smile on her face.

"Didn't your mama always tell you breakfast is the most important meal of the day?" she asked.

"Possibly yes. But I most likely wasn't listening very closely." Baza smiled, wiped his mouth with the paper towel napkin she offered him, and pushed back from the table. "I've gotta go. My car is here." He kissed her forehead. "Thank you, I really mean it."

Nevertheless, Baza was always happy for any excuse to travel that took him out of New York and away from the office for even a couple of days.

But when he got back, taking a taxi directly from LaGuardia to the office, Baza found Big Bird waiting with eager anticipation to tell him about 25 more mortgage-backed security issues that he had closed with a raft of investment bankers. He was also burbling about a new study on the housing market. Now well aware of Baza's mounting worries about a housing bubble, Big Bird had taken to shoveling reassuring studies and articles in his direction.

Almost as an afterthought, Big Bird finally asked, "How was the conference? Did they tell you the world is coming to an end?"

"They didn't have to," retorted Baza, who wasn't in the mood for Big Bird's taunting boosterism.

"Well, I've got something here that might put your mind at ease. Lehman just paid Webster Associates one hundred K to dig into market conditions—I mean really dig, going all the way down to the grassroots level. They interviewed real estate agents in every metro area."

That is liking asking terrorists for advice on how to orchestrate a peaceful protest march, Baza thought.

"Real estate agents?" Baza actually replied. "C'mon, Mayberry. You know what they're like. They're commissioned salespeople who wake up every morning without a job. If they're not drunk with optimism, they can't function."

"Yeah, well, this also looks at the demographics and the current literature. Read it for yourself. When you connect all the dots, it sure looks like the market's gonna continue to expand," said Big Bird, tossing the document in Baza's direction.

Reports with a similar veneer of credibility were circulating throughout Wall Street. Everybody read them, and almost everybody wanted to believe them. Meanwhile, high-profile industry shills, like the chief economist at the National Association of Real Estate Professionals, kept issuing rosy predictions illustrated by authoritative-looking charts and graphs.

It was all too reminiscent of the dot-com boom, when some wishful thinkers declared the "death of the business cycle" shortly before the crash. It had only been six years since that bubble had burst, Baza thought. Hadn't anybody learned anything?

He and Big Bird cut the tension with a few moments of company gossip. After sharing stories of how Hank Herman got fired and why Frances Ellender was moving to Berlin and leaving the U.S. for good, Baza broached the topic he really wanted to talk about.

"Listen, I've read a hundred studies like this piece of crap," he said, pushing the impressive-looking document aside. "As I said before, I really think we need to go for lower ratings on these packages stuffed for subprime loans, especially the option ARMs and two-twenty-eights."

They had moved from the office over to the bar at the Ritz as they talked. Baza finally felt prepared to take the heat from Big Bird, who glared as he took a big slug of his Scotch and grabbed a fistful of mixed nuts from the bowl in front of them. These he shoveled into his mouth all at once, crunching noisily as half-chewed fragments crumbled onto his chin, blue blazer and tie. Baza was so distracted by this mess that he was finally driven to reach over with a napkin and brush him off. Big Bird looked down and said, "Thanks, mom."

"This is a huge problem whether you realize it or not, Michael. I believe the housing market is turning, and turning quickly. We would be insane to keep giving out these ratings. They are dishonest, not to mention downright absurd," said Baza, whose voice now kept rising; the whole bar could hear him. People at the other tables looked over to see what was causing the ruckus.

"Don't believe everything you hear, my friend," Big Bird broke in, the flicker of a sneer playing on his face. For a second Baza was stopped short by the sarcastic remark, but then went on even more forcefully without skipping another beat.

"Look at us! We're pathetic! Moody's is supposed to be the eyes and the ears of investors. But all we do is chase revenue and profits. It's our job to sound the alarm on bad deals. We're the guardians of the hen house, except we're totally in cahoots with the foxes who pay us." Baza drained the rest of his Scotch and motioned to the bartender for the same.

"Anyway, who set things up so that we're paid by the investment banks instead of the investors? What a stupid, corrupt system...and what a monster it's created."

"You're beating a sad, lone drum my friend. Do you think we're big enough to fix the system that created this?" Big Bird shook his head.

"The housing market is going to collapse because we became too greedy. And don't pretend you don't know it, Mayberry, because I can't believe you're that stupid."

"Chicken Little will be the one left with nothing on her plate. Grow a pair!" Big Bird snapped, becoming increasingly annoyed by Baza's rising fury.

"Open your eyes! Foreclosures are skyrocketing. Millions of people will be thrown out of their homes. And you and I will have blood on our hands, my little Irish friend. Before long, the days of five or six or seven million home transactions a year will be nothing more than a distant memory. And has it ever occurred to you that when the mortgage-backed securities market dies, so will Moody's? There's no quick fix for this—no way to pump it up with your bogus studies and rah-rah rhetoric. Do you have a clue as to what I am talking about here?" Baza demanded, finally coming up for air.

This was the first time Baza had so totally exposed his professional fears and his related personal anxiety. He hesitated for a moment, but then charged ahead. The more he got off his chest, the more the anxiety seemed to dissipate.

"Mark my words, our country will face an economic calamity of epic proportions because of the rotten system we've helped to perpetuate. The only good news is that, once the system is de-leveraged and we purge all these toxic loans, the collapse might help us return to our senses. I mean, imagine, if you will," Baza continued, "a country where personal values and public policies favor savings over irrational debt and promote investment instead of speculation...a place where people don't believe greed is good and consumption is the way to happiness." Baza was on a roll, channeling years of resentment over the way America had squandered its prosperity. The sense of entitlement, the forty-year consumption binge, the astounding amount of waste—it all mingled with his disgust with himself and came out in one angry rush.

For once in his life, Big Bird was speechless. He looked up with a blank expression that suggested Baza's rant might have struck some inner chord with him, whether he admitted it or not. Except Big Bird was already too drunk to notice how Baza's point of view shifted. Midway through his outburst, Baza became an outsider looking in at the United States and its shallow, materialistic culture. Although he had lived in the U.S. for twenty years, he could still switch sides and play the observer, judging the nation as though he were not part of it. His language made it obvious: "You" instead of "we," "there" instead of "here," and "your country," implying that it wasn't his. With this unconscious defense mechanism, Baza distanced himself from blame.

Having taken himself out of the picture, Baza now went in for the attack. "Debt drove this trend—debt that you wanted in the worst way for me to rate AAA, and which I did.

"All this bloated borrowing, and for what? Expensive bling? Monster SUVs? Vacations in cheesy tropical resorts? Why earn and save for it when you can borrow and get it today? Nobody cares if you can really afford it or not... Hell, Mayberry, you know the figures as well as I do. A savings rate of less than one percent. Credit-card debt, almost a trillion dollars. Mortgage debt, now more than eleven trillion dollars. You and I made that happen, man. We are the leaders of the debt parade."

Baza started to sweat visibly as his language went back from "you" and "them" to "we" and "me."

"My group rated every piece of shit you sent our way, giving Wall Street license to pile more and more debt onto companies, individuals and small businesses. Take those home equity deals we rated AA. It used to be that home equity was your safety net...or the stash you built up to pay for your kid's college or start a business. Now it's a piggybank you can raid to buy depreciating assets, like cars, boats and trips but nobody had the courage to call 'bullshit,' because the fees were just too good."

Baza took another deep breath and then dropped the bomb.

"Big Bird, you and I are guilty of helping to create this disaster, and by my estimation we will each serve not less than ten years in prison.

Mayberry's only discernible reaction was to chuckle and shake his head. This annoyed Baza greatly. He finished by folding his arms across his chest. "This whole thing is going to crater and I refuse to be a part of it."

He stopped himself just short of saying: "Tomorrow is the day I come clean. I am going into the office to adjust our MBS models and I promise you, there will be no more AAA ratings coming from our shop." Because, in truth, he wondered if he really would.

Big Bird was silent. Baza thought he was taking a minute to cool down. He stared as if his eyes were lasers that could bore right through Baza's skull, then turned to the bartender with a cool expression.

"Norman, how about getting another pop for both of us. While you're are at it, get this guy an AK-47 so he can go on an insane rampage, killing everyone in the bar, the restaurant and the lounge, and then move out onto Central Park South, mow down some tourists and kill all of the horses pulling those cute carriages. Then we can all read about this crazed immigrant on Page Six of the Post tomorrow."

Icy sarcasm was the first phase of any serious attack by Big Bird, a sure sign of the nuclear conflagration to follow.

"In less than an hour, a CNN truck will be parked outside this hotel and experts will explain why the good go bad, the sane go loco, and rich immigrants going nuts in Gringoland is a growing trend."

The muscles in Big Bird's jaw twitched, and his tone became menacing. "What the fuck got into you? Are you taking meth? Did your father jump off a bridge? Or has your body been taken over by pod people from another planet?"

Baza wished he had kept up his old habit of wearing a rubber band on his wrist. Once, years ago, he had read a story about people who were phobic about flying and would snap a rubber band on their wrists when they began getting anxious. The idea was that the sting would snap them out of their irrational fears. He tried it, and it seemed to help him pull himself back when he was teetering on the edge of one of his panic attacks. He could have used that sting now.

Instead, he said, "Excuse me," and trotted downstairs to the restroom.

The restrooms at the Ritz were of all gleaming marble, expensive wood, and the scent of lemon verbena. Thick cotton towels were stacked in an intricately woven bamboo basket. Baza leaned down and checked to make sure the stalls were empty. He walked into the corner stall and banged his forehead on the metal door three times. That was an alternative to the rubber band.

Between the alcohol, the head-banging and Big Bird's impending atomic rage, Baza was becoming unglued.

He looked at himself in the mirror, smiled and said, "You are a good man." He didn't really believe it, but saying the words gave him some relief from the unfolding drama.

Calming the noise in his head was no easy matter. His thoughts were mixed up, like an overturned garbage can on the street. As he walked up the stairs, he thought that his speech was persuasive and imagined Big Bird agreeing with him, perhaps even helping him explain the situation to his boss, Dana Fielding, and her boss, Patrick O'Dell, another crazed Irishman. But by the time he reached the landing at the top, he was sure Big Bird would be screaming for his head.

Baza was scrambling for a way to begin righting the wrongs so evident at Moody's. Big Bird was clearly not the right person to go to for help, but he was the one feeding the funnel that had to be plugged or at least slowed down. Baza knew his team was operating with old information and an obsolete model. It was delusional, destructive and had to be stopped.

When he got back to the bar, Big Bird was gone.

Written on a napkin next to his drinks were these words:

"Take these wild ideas to your boss, and don't ever, ever again cross the line by sharing the inner workings of your models with me. It violates company policy and you know it." "Well," thought Baza, "At least I know what lies he's going to trot out."

At that moment, his iPhone rang. When he answered, Big Bird's voice said, "Just so you know, I did not hear a thing you said because the bar was too loud." Baza ended the call without a word.

He turned to Norman, hoping for some distracting small talk, but the bartender was busy describing his recent heart attack to another customer.

Baza chewed at his fingernails, which were already down to the nub, and looked around. In horror, he suddenly began to imagine that some competitor or, worse still, a regulator had overheard their conversation and was already reporting it. Perhaps Big Bird had spotted the Feds; that might even have been what prompted him to flee. Like water filling a cup from a dispenser, his paranoia was steadily rising.

Feeling in need of some shred of positive human contact, he turned to a couple sitting at the bar next to him. They looked to be in their late fifties and were clearly decked out for the evening. "Headed to a show?" he asked.

"We are going to *Mama Mia* and then to David's for dinner. Have you been there?" asked the woman. Her Tahitian black pearls were bunched up in the hollow under her wrinkled neck.

"Oh yes, it's fantastic. Between the food, the wine list and the setting, it's one of the best in New York."

"Is it expensive?" asked the man. He was wearing a three-piece suit, a get-up rarely seen in New York except when worn by gay hipsters in Chelsea.

"Well, yes, I'd say it is. Where are you folks from?"

"Ohio. We're celebrating Bob's promotion at First Columbus Bank; he was made Executive Vice President last month. He led the mortgage operation for the last five years. The bank was so thrilled with the revenue and profit growth...now he's getting the rewards." The woman cast a classic adoring-wife look in Bob's direction.

Baza came to attention, as if he were an investigative reporter. "Congratulations. Just out of curiosity, how's the housing market doing back there, by the way?"

"Compared to the rest of the country, not so hot. But Ohio does not have the ups and downs you folks have in New York and in California, it's a lot more stable," said the wife.

"The economy is weakening because the auto companies and other industrials aren't doing well," Bob explained. "But we got a boost from low mortgage rates and some innovative loans we have been pushing the last few years. Those subprime products gave us a real boost."

"Really," said Baza. "How are they working out?"

"Well, Sarah here thinks they are a time bomb, but our CEO loves them and so does the board. I pushed them harder than most of the local banks and we picked up market share and posted a record year," Bob said with a satisfied smile.

"Can you imagine, home loans with nothing down? A fixed rate for only two years for someone with poor credit? I think those guys have rocks in their head," said Sarah.

"We were worried at first, but then Wall Street began buying them like crazy. They took the risk off our balance sheet and asked us to underwrite more of them. So we are originating them as fast we can," added Bob. "And what do you do, young man?"

"I work on Wall Street in the CDO market."

"CDOs?" repeated Sarah quizzically. "I don't know what that is, but it sounds important. Are you from New York?"

"It stands for credit default obligations—pretty boring stuff, but I do well enough. My native country is Honduras, but I've lived in New York for years. I love it here." Baza felt relieved to be having a normal conversation with normal people.

"Time to scoot, sweetie," said Bob, clutching Sarah's arm as he pulled out three twenty-dollar bills from his wallet to pay Norman. "Can you believe they get $21 for a martini?"

As Norman made change, he winked at Sarah. "If you ever dump Mr. Handsome here, come back and spend the weekend with me in the Big Apple. You promise?"

Sarah blushed and said, "Oh Norman, you're so sweet."

Norman waited until they were out the door, then caught Baza's eye and shook his head.

"Your pal was breathing fire when he left. Is he OK?

"Yeah, too much stress at work. He'll be all right." Baza answered flatly.

"You know, I've known Michael for twenty-five years, and I have seen him in some ugly pickles...with his bosses, girls at the bar and even obnoxious customers. But lately he seems more wound up than usual. He sure let loose tonight...sorry it was at your expense.

"I appreciate that Norman, but I'll be fine," said Baza.

"You know what worried me tonight? That AK-47 stuff. I mean, what was he talking about? We have the President of Colombia in the hotel tonight, and two of his secret service agents were at the bar. They were off duty, but they heard him ranting about killing people and it totally freaked them out. They even went to see the hotel manager. So of course, he comes and asks me if Mike was square. I told him he was fine, a good customer for years. But with these hotshot Wall Street types, you never know what might set them off." Norman finished polishing his glasses.

The place had emptied out, and Norman leaned his elbows on the bar, settling in for some chat. Even after half a night's work at the bar, Baza noticed his white shirt was still starched and immaculate, and that he was wearing gold cufflinks from Cartier. He wondered how he afforded them on a bartender's salary.

"I remember one night, a guy from Bear Stearns shoved Shen Sui—you know her, the cocktail waitress, beautiful girl—and he started ranting about 'the assholes at the SEC.'

"He was way out there, I'll tell you, veins in his neck all popped out, knocking glasses off the table, flailing around. The whole time he's complaining about how unfair things are on Wall Street...Yeah, right. I bleed for ya, buddy."

"Sounds like he could have been a few guys I know," Baza chuckled.

"Yeah? Anyway, the Bear Stearns lawyers convinced the hotel it would be bad PR to take him to court. They settled with Sui. Between you and me, we all told her she should hire a tough lawyer and take them to the cleaners. Never saw the wacko again..."

"Is that right?" Baza offered.

"I have to say, Baza….some of you Wall Street guys get wound pretty tight. Take care of Mike, or better yet, avoid him if you think he's unraveling. If he does, I have a feeling it won't be pretty."

"Will do, man." Baza was half-listening as he tapped on his iPhone, seeking an antidote for his anxiety and continual thoughts of Trina. He decided to quit fighting them and finally texted her: *You free later?* Then he ordered a tequila shot from Norman and scanned his emails. His assistant, Jennifer, a redhead with a puritanical work ethic, messaged with two attachments, asking for his approval on two new issues totaling $1.2 billion. She needed an answer by 8 a.m.

He phoned her number. "Hi...right, no problem with those issues. I'll sign off in the morning, just put them on my desk. In the meantime, want to meet me for a drink? I'm at the Ritz, we could catch up."

"Sure, if you need to talk. But I was sort of planning to meet Phil. It's the one-year anniversary of our first date." Jennifer seemed to be on the perennial hunt for a husband.

"No problem, we'll chat in the morning. Maybe you could also block out a couple of hours to spend some time with me on the models. I've been thinking about making some changes," Baza said.

"What kind of changes, Baza?" Jennifer had a note of alarm in her voice. "I'm sure we've got this right. I mean, we're already so risk-averse. We've been over it a dozen times... Has Bunting been getting to you, like he does every time you go through London?" she said, almost pleading with him to forget the idea.

Her tone made Baza worry more. One sign of being in denial is when you need others to join you there.

"Maybe so, I just want to talk about certain elements, like the home price projections. You know, make sure that we are on solid ground. We can't ignore the volatility we're seeing."

"Ok boss, let's chat in the morning."

Baza loved it when she called him boss; she did it in a way that showed respect and affection at the same time. He was fond of her, partly because she was as capable as she was good-natured.

Once or twice he was even tempted to give her a glimpse behind the curtain of his private life, but thought better of it."

"OK, bye, Jennifer."

"Wait! I forgot to ask you... Did you see Mike tonight? Andrea told me that he came into his office screaming on his phone, slamming doors and kicking furniture around. Everyone in the outer office could hear him. They couldn't make out exactly what he was saying, except he kept shouting, 'that motherfucker.'"

12

Baza walked East on Central Park South, then wound his way over to 55th Street and into the King Cole Bar at the St. Regis. In the cool New York twilight, the sky was color of the Caribbean Sea on a sunny day. It was *l'heure bleu*, the hour of love. He was dying to see Trina. But he was trying to keep himself from calling her as long as he could. He didn't want to betray his excitement to her for fear he might completely lose control of himself. He took a seat at the bar and ordered a double single malt Scotch and tried to take the edge off of his anxiety. He chatted with the bartender for a while before turning his attention to his phone and finally giving in and texting her.

Ready when you are. He waited for what felt like an interminable length of time for her to reply, but once he checked his watch he realized it had only been ten minutes. He wondered if it was possible he was already losing a grip on just about everything in his life.

They agreed to meet in 30 minutes at her studio on Rivington Street. He walked to Lexington, hopped onto the Number 6 train, found a seat in the corner and stared at the continuing education ads over the windows. He could feel the alcohol coursing through his system.

His heartbeat accelerated as he transferred to the F train and got closer to the East Broadway Station. The sense of descending into a pit of desire and danger was his form of foreplay. He walked the four blocks to her building and rang the buzzer. He had texted her when he came out of the subway and so she buzzed him straight in.

Baza's fears rarely focused on the true risks of a situation, like being robbed or getting busted for soliciting a prostitute. Instead he would obsess over some far-fetched, imagined scenario that the police would finger him for, embroidering the scene with frightening details as he replayed it over and over in his mind. He would picture his fingerprints on the doorknob, his image on the video, the police reading the text messages on his cellphone—a damning confluence of details adding up to a verdict of "guilty as charged."

Trina opened the door wearing a red satin robe and heels which accented every curve and detail of her gorgeous legs. She waved him in, kissed him and went to her makeshift bar on top of a sideboard to pour them drinks.

"Hi baby, why you been a stranger?" She poured them both single malt Scotch, his up and hers on the rocks.

Baza took off his jacket and tie and drank in the scent of her Opium cologne combined with some sort of bergamot and eucalyptus aromatherapy oils that seemed to be emanating from a small dish with a candle underneath it that sat on the table. Her studio was small and cramped but neat and the familiar smells made him feel oddly at home. There was a tiny kitchen, more like a closet big enough to stand and turn around in, off to one side, and a bathroom of equal dimensions.

"Busy, traveling. I have no life. I think I mentioned that part before." Baza shrugged and smiled.

"I thought you don't like me anymore baby," Trina pouted and handed him his drink, rubbing up against him briefly, then pulling away. Trina had perfected the art of teasing Baza and this dance would go on between them for a while, which was just exactly how he liked it. He wasn't sure if he was fooling himself that he meant anything to her other than being just another John, another of one of her many sources of income. He felt like an idiot for even letting the thought permeate his consciousness. But there it was.

"Not you, just my crazy life," Baza said, as he pulled her towards him, running his hand down her sinewy back muscles until he found her perfectly round ass which he cupped each hand around, encircling each side. She purred, kissed him, then walked away to flounce into a wide-fanned wicker chair in the corner that looked like it belonged on the veranda of a southern riverside home, not in an overcrowded apartment on the Lower East Side.

Trina seemed a bit more removed than when he had seen her last and wondered if she really had been offended by his absence.

"How have things been with you?" Baza suddenly felt awkward for asking, as if he were breaching their unspoken contract. He genuinely wanted to know, though, so he held her gaze and waited till she spoke. She studied her red lacquered nails for a moment, then waved them in front of her face.

"Nothing darling, it's not your problem. Cheers!" She picked up her glass of Scotch and threw it back in one gulp.

"Tell me, what is it?"

"Nah, just.... it'll all be fine."

"Trina, just tell me. I'm...your friend, okay?"

"This building is being bought out by a bigger landlord—everyone has to move."

"Oh, well maybe that's a good thing? I mean, this place is kind of small. Will you get a settlement?"

"A bit," she shrugged. "Pocket change."

"How much?" Baza asked.

Trina got up, opened a drawer in the sideboard, took out a letter and handed it to him. Baza scanned it quickly.

"Ten thousand? That's not bad!"

"What's 10 G gonna get me in this city? Besides I already got credit card debt to pay off."

"Trina, you do realize you can buy an apartment in this city with almost no money down?" Baza suddenly had a flash of inspiration.

"What are you talkin' about? I couldn't possibly afford to buy anywhere here. Maybe I'll move to Florida. I got a cousin there."

"This is the era of cheap money we're living in. No reason why you shouldn't benefit from it either."

"What do you mean?"

"I mean. There's no reason why you can't get a mortgage—even with less than $10,000 as a down payment." He hesitated, realizing he was about to make a huge leap. "Maybe I can help you with part of it."

She smiled coyly at him. "Baby, you'd do that for me? I couldn't!" She waved him away but giggled, but then went suddenly serious. "Listen, how do you think someone like me is gonna qualify for a freaking mortgage? I don't exactly have pay stubs in my line of work. Cash is king, baby."

"Leave it to me. I'll make some inquiries. You're not going to be on the street or in some shitty excuse for a cockroach-infested apartment." He walked over to her, put out his hand and pulled her out of the chair and kissed her, running his hands up and down her body, his excitement growing. It was sexual combined with the illicit pleasure of finding some way to do some good for her that involved gaming the system he was charged to represent. He knew it was risky and a house of cards, but he'd have to find a way to set her up. He felt charged with a new mission.

He woke with a start at 3 a.m. to see her sleeping next to him, his body curled around hers. He felt a sudden sense of the familiar panic returning, uncoiled himself, dressed quickly and slipped out. He left a wad of cash on her dresser for her, at the same time telling himself this was purely a professional relationship.

After finding a cab that whisked him back uptown, he found his addled, booze-soaked brain going down the usual path of what-ifs and exploring all the likely ways his follies might be exposed, such as his calls being traced, his emails and text messages being read, and the movement of certain funds being tracked, as had happened to New York Governor Eliot Spitzer.

The Feds, the local police, the DEA—you could name any agency or authority, and Baza could build a storyline about his being ensnared in some mortifying situation with a transsexual, not just your typical hooker, but a chick with a dick. Yet at the same time, a part of him didn't even care anymore. It was as if he was willing his inevitable decline just to come on already.

The next morning, Baza found two of his senior analysts, Henry Kaplan and Sandra Cherovich, waiting for him as he approached the entrance to Moody's headquarters. They looked nervous standing outside in the cold, which made Baza feel the same way. Kaplan, who liked to play the clown, twisted his wool scarf around his neck when he saw Baza walking towards them, miming a hangman's noose.

The auditors who were conducting ongoing monitoring of securities were apparently picking up the pace of their investigations. The office buzz was that they would be requesting interviews with various members of Baza's team over the next few days.

"Baza, we can't mess around with this anymore. We've got to update the assumptions and revise the model," said Kaplan. "Everything's going to hit the fan if we don't."

"Yes, but the whole house of cards will fall down if we do," Baza said, kicking himself for backtracking on his stance last night with Big Bird. He quickly qualified his statement. "I know you're right. I'm just saying, we could trigger a chain reaction and do we really want to do that?

"I think the data is screaming at us to do something," Henry replied. "We've been saying for *months* that the model we're using is antiquated, obsolete, a total dinosaur in the context of the market now. Subprime was *nothing* when this model was constructed. Now it's *huge*. Everybody in the *world* is a homeowner, it seems—except Sandy and me, of course—and half of 'em seem to be in trouble."

Henry Kaplan looked over at Sandra who nodded emphatically. "I'm with him, but I'm also freezing! Can't we go inside?" she pleaded.

"You're right about the model, of course, but it's a question of timing, meaning when we introduce the adjustments. We really have to think it through." Baza said.

He was embarrassed by his answer. Henry could be a whiner, but he and Sandra both knew their way around sophisticated modeling techniques. They were professionals, and he was giving them the corporate shuffle. It made him sick. But he also knew that an overnight adjustment in the model would kill the mortgage-backed securities market. It would be like the meteor that caused the great dinosaur die-off, leaving only the crater.

In the end, he and his colleagues knew—any analyst worthy of the name would have known—that Moody's models were riddled with faulty assumptions. They did not adequately account for the risk of subprime loans. They relied on historic foreclosure data, ignoring how lax profit-hungry loan originators had become with their loan terms and underwriting standards. And they ignored clear signs of deterioration in the housing market, including rising defaults, growing losses, and dwindling cash flow from mortgage payments.

There was more: Moody's used the standard Monte Carlo simulations of macroeconomic variables to model losses—another case of "too much history, not enough reality," as Sandy put it. The model assumed most loans were typical mortgages with typical borrowers—not exotic subprime loans made to borrowers with shaky credit. Not to mention the refi problem. In monitoring loan packages, no one tracked the individual properties to see whether additional loans were taken out on them, socking borrowers with debt that not only exceeded the value of the house, but pushed payments higher than they could afford.

Roger Jordoin had contacted Baza the day before with yet another concern. His group had been making inquiries with several lenders, and the feedback was scary. The auditors realized that speculation was a much bigger factor in loan portfolios than Moody's had been told. A large share of the properties had been bought by flippers, not by owner-occupants. Jordoin was questioning the entire portfolio mix.

Baza had parted ways with Kaplan and Cherovich in the elevator as he stayed on to pay Jordoin a visit. Now sitting with him in his office, Baza spotted a small box of rubber bands on Jordoin's desk, helped himself to one and put it on his wrist. The other man didn't seem to notice as he stared at his spreadsheets with his brow deeply furrowed.

Normally not one to emote, Jordoin was visibly angry. "What the hell are you guys doing down there? This is a huge mess we've uncovered, and I'm going to hold you responsible. What were you thinking, Baza?"

"Hold on there, chief," said Baza, holding up his palm theatrically. "It's not my team that's making these loans; you know that. We rely on the data that Merrill and the rest of them give us. If they say the properties are owner-occupied, we go with that. If that's not the real story, it's certainly not my team's fault," retorted Baza.

He could feel the blame game unfolding, with earnings, revenue and reputations at stake.

"Oh, come on! There is a lot more to it than whether properties are owner-occupied or not. Did you guys go to business school or barber's college? Your assumptions about price elasticity and borrower behavior were totally off the mark. Why didn't you adjust your models?" Jordoin sputtered. "While I'm at it, what about this crazy stuff your pal Mayberry is trying to sell?"

"What are you talking about?" Baza snapped back.

"Is it true you were going to rate those index securities AAA? They're pure junk!"

"What stuff?" Baza was stunned that the audit group was somehow clued into Mayberry's doings and he suddenly wondered what else they knew.

Jordoin said nothing but walked towards his office door, signaling an end to the meeting.

When Baza got back to his office, he learned that Fielding had set up an emergency meeting for that afternoon in an off-site conference room. He was scheduled to give her a two-hour debriefing over lunch. *Two hours for what*, he thought. Baza was sure that all along she'd known everything they had been doing. He didn't understand how there could be any big secret that would take two hours to explain. Baza felt as though the earth was starting to slide and crumble beneath his feet.

"The agenda is as follows," she wrote in the Outlook scheduling email. "First, let's look at the problem deals that Audit identified, then review your latest proposal for adjustments to the model. Then we can see what exposure you feel the firm may have as it pertains to these audited pools. Does that make sense? Who on your team will you be bringing? Also, please bring any new housing market forecasts that your team is looking over."

Baza replied, "We will be ready. I'll bring Sandra—she's the one who's been closest to the modeling discussions—and Kaplan, too. Should we bring in Legal? I'm not sure my team is equipped to sort out 'exposure.'"

He hit the "send" button and thought, *Yeah, we're ready. But for what?*

When Baza got to the meeting with Fielding he felt ridiculous for asking whether Legal should be brought into the meeting. Lawyers were running the meeting.

It was clear from the start that the meeting was an inquisition, not a collaboration. Naturally, Fielding had invited legal counsel—not only two in-house attorneys, but also two outside lawyers from the firm of Richards, Inman and Speers. Randall Meeks was an Ichabod Crane type, tall, lanky and taciturn, with a steely gaze. Roberta Rich was built like a fireplug, said almost nothing, and took copious notes on everything.

To Baza's surprise, Meeks ran the meeting. He jumped right in with a series of rapid-fire questions about the way Baza's group handled the tracking of market trends and correction of the model.

At first, the tone of the questions was matter of fact, but quickly became prosecutorial. Meeks began looking agitated. "Here's what I want to know," he demanded. "Is it that you didn't fully understand these dangerous trends? Or did you simply choose to ignore them for the purposes of your analysis?"

"This feels like a witch hunt," Sandra, who was sitting next to Baza, scrawled on a corner of her legal pad, pushing it in the Honduran's direction.

He looked at her, nodded, and whispered, "It's OK. They're just doing their job, as we've done for the last year."

In truth, he was a nervous wreck and his head felt ready to explode. Just then, a text message came through from Trina. *Thanks for last night, you were great. XOXO.*

Suddenly Baza was struck by the absurdity of it all. Here he was in America, trying to help his family leverage its fortune, and the entire concept of financial leverage was being revealed as destructive, at least when applied by the wrong hands.

Things were not what they seemed—not at the TS bars, and not at Moody's, either; nor at lending and investment banking institutions all across the country.

Most of the discussion revolved around the group's home price projections, which turned out to be the most pivotal input to the model. If home prices decline and people owe more on their mortgages than the property is worth, why wouldn't they just walk away?

Thinking of his father, who would never tell a lie or cheat on his taxes, it occurred to Baza that bailing on a mortgage obligation was right in tune with America's culture of hyper-competition and self-absorption. Honor, reputation, responsibility—these were nice ideas, but when money was on the table, people figured they had to take care of themselves. They knew nobody else would.

Meeks' brittle, insistent voice cut through Baza's musings. "Was there any consideration that home prices might fall? And if so, shouldn't that have been a more important factor in the model?"

"Of course we considered that, but the prevailing wisdom held that home prices might conceivably go flat, but would not fall. For that reason, the model did not consider falling prices," Baza explained, trying hard not to seem defensive.

"Well, they *are* falling. We spend millions of dollars every year on market studies, databases, housing reports, conferences. Shouldn't we have anticipated that possibility, at least?" Meeks said, not looking at Baza, but staying fixed on the spreadsheets he had laid out in front of him.

What bothered Baza most of all was the suggestion that he had no idea what he was doing. It was one thing to be judged as a villain, a bad guy, somebody who crossed the line, another to be judged an idiot. He glanced over at Sandra. Her face was a mask of dismay. It sent shivers down his spine.

He was suddenly overwhelmed by the sensation that everything he thought he had, everything he'd worked for, was falling apart. It was like the potted orchid Sandra had given him during the holidays. It was an exquisite white blossom and stayed that way for weeks. Then one morning he got up to find a bare stem and petals scattered on the floor.

He caught Dana Fielding's eye. She looked pale and gaunt, as well.

Fielding made an attempt to take charge. "OK, let's remember, this meeting is not about assigning blame. That's not relevant. We judged the market based on the best thinking and the best information we had; it just happens we called it wrong—like just about everybody else, I might add.

"The question is, how are we going to adapt the model to changing market conditions going forward? What are we going to do going forward?" Fielding straightened her blouse and fiddled with her left earring.

At this show of support, Baza jumped in to challenge Meeks. "You know, we're not stupid here. We have already factored in much more conservative home price scenarios and payment projections, and therefore much higher foreclosure rates.

"We have been running these new scenarios all week, testing them on three pending packages that the bankers and salespeople are very anxious to get out into the marketplace. Based on the results, nothing in these packages can be rated any higher than Ba1," concluded Baza, "And I can assure you, that's something the company does not like to hear."

There was dead silence in the room for at least 20 seconds, which felt like an hour to Baza.

"And we know what that means, don't we?" interjected Sandra in a cocky tone. "They can't go to market with a Ba1, which means there is no market." Suddenly emboldened, she added, "So, what now, guys?"

Another 15 seconds went by before Fielding pushed back her chair and said, "I think I have everything I need for my meeting with the executive team this afternoon," she said. "One last question, Baza. Is your team prepared to turn these adaptations in the model into a full-blown recommendation?"

"Yes," said Baza. "I did that more or less a year ago, then again six months ago, and then 30 days ago. I just didn't do it formally—sorry."

As if under a spell, every person in the room got up and pulled out a Blackberry, reading messages or tapping out new ones. Baza automatically started counting smiles but quickly gave up. There were more worried looks than chirpy ones. In fact, he realized he had not seen a cheerful person at Moody's in months.

"Baza, can I see you in my office after we finish here?" asked Fielding.

He walked down the hall to Fielding's office, but was having a difficult time putting one foot ahead of the other. He felt nearly paralyzed with fear. If the recommendations he had just made were implemented, it could bring the entire housing market to a standstill, instantly fill bankers' balance sheets with bad debts, maybe even cause some kind of meltdown in the financial system.

Fielding's admin, Deirdre, showed Baza to a chair in the inner office and said Fielding would be back shortly. Dazed, he did not even hear her offer him something to drink.

"We have a real mess on our hands, don't we?" said Fielding as she walked in and slumped wearily in her office chair.

"I suspect that some big changes will be underway in your group. Before anything else happens, I just wanted to thank you for all that you have done for this company and for me over the last eighteen months—I mean that sincerely. You brought a new degree of professionalism and integrity to this operation.

"If, for some reason, MBS offerings decline in this environment, I just want you to know that Moody's will find a place for you," she said as she stared out the window.

Baza was having trouble interpreting her corporate-speak. Was this goodbye, thanks, get lost...what did it mean?

Never having worked for a big company before, he hadn't realized how ill-equipped they were for a crisis. They are built to grow, not to contract; to burnish their reputations, not drag them through the dirt. Everything in corporate life is organized to keep negatives under control and disaster at bay.

When systems fail and the crisis comes, the corporate play-books offer no guidance. No one is ready. You can practice the Heimlich maneuver over and over again on a plastic dummy, but when the 80-year old man at the next table is choking on his bite of a cheeseburger, you flinch and wonder what to do. Call 911? Crush the frail old man's chest? Yell for a doctor? Some people have cool heads and seem to know just what to do, but most do not.

What remains operative through times of crisis is the instinct for self-preservation, which rushes into the breach, overwhelming every other personal and organizational consideration. Of course, self-interest also rules when companies are moving up the success curve. But in those situations, people see the rewards for acting like part of the team.

When there are no more rewards and only blame to be allocated, people act like contestants in some corporate version of *Survivor*, the mother of all reality TV shows. They defend, deflect, hide, lash out—do whatever it takes to protect what they have.

Those are the kinds of situations that give rise to a speech like Fielding's. What she said was one thing, but what she meant was something more sinister.

Baza had a feeling what she was really saying was *you're on your own, buddy, so good luck*. He was already certain his future was bleak. In fact, you could say that in some ways, he had been preparing for it his entire life. It was all too easy for him to picture himself as the object of public scrutiny, blame, humiliation and even criminal charges.

He gave Fielding a warm two-handed handshake and left.

When he got to his office, Sandra and Kaplan were waiting expectantly. "What now?" asked Kaplan with an oh-shit smile.

"Just do your job," Baza said flatly, feeling numbed by every-thing that had transpired over the past couple of hours.

"Uh, sure. We have twenty deals pending. You want to run them on the old model or the new model?" asked Kaplan.

"We have only one approved model, run it on that."

Their eyes met in silent understanding that what they were doing was wrong. There is a right way to do wrong, but that's not what they were doing. Kaplan left the room without another word.

Baza thought of the huge investment losses his father sustained as a result of the U.S. savings and loan debacle of the 1980s and '90s. He wondered if his father had felt the same way he did now. Could it be that a tendency to get mixed up in these sorts of disasters was genetic?

Nevertheless, he went online and scrolled through the downtown apartment and condo sale listings. He found a few one-bedroom options and picked up the phone to call the brokers to make some appointments to view them the next day. His half-baked plan was to view a few himself, narrow down the choices, then bring Trina along and have her pick the one she liked best. Then come what may.

13

Moody's had begun revising the model it used to rate subprime mortgages, but the process was stalled.

Meanwhile, the lumbering, sluggish apparatus for oversight and regulation of the financial services industry had finally roused. The Securities and Exchange Commission, Congressional committees, the FBI, banking regulators—now they were all intent on pulling back the sheets to reveal how rating agencies fomented the housing market crash.

Not so many months ago, Baza had been an avid reader of the blogs, but now they turned his stomach. Like buzzards feasting on carrion, they couldn't get enough of the subprime fiasco. Amateur journalists and social critics were busy composing searing headlines: "Find the subprime bums and throw them in jail."

As for the professional news organizations, their coverage had become a maddening drumbeat that echoed in Baza's brain. He subscribed to a free Google service that hourly forwarded to him any publication, website, or blog that made reference to Moody's, "MBS investigations," "rating agency scandals," or any one of two dozen other keyword combinations. Among them he had included his own name, half-waiting for the dreaded headline: "Head of MBS Analytics Arrested in Transsexual Prostitution Raid."

Roger Jordoin, head of Moody's audit group, was subpoenaed to testify, as was Ralph Torrent, the CEO. Fielding was also asked to be in attendance, but not to sit at the grill table, where so many corporate executives had been pelted with Congressional rants and taunts. Members of Congress are not subject to slander or libel laws, so they can say whatever they want in public, and often do.

The industry's reliance on credit scores proved to be another bad bet. When people had negative equity in a home, little invested, and big loan payments hanging over their heads, abandoning their homes and mortgages was a rational economic choice. Their past behavior and resulting credit scores had nothing to do with it.

In a way, Baza had been right all along. After a few years in the U.S., he had observed a shift in the culture—a breakdown in the old order of personal honor, institutional responsibility, and the rule of law. The trouble started long before anyone ever heard of a subprime loan.

While at Dartmouth, he had taken a class on criminology and read about what happened when Mexico had lost the rule of law. The same problem had been happening for years in the urban ghettos of the U.S. Lawlessness has a way of being contagious.

If the mayor is known to be corrupt and the police are beating up on citizens, is it any surprise that people double-park with impunity? Once trust is broken, the effect keeps rippling outward.

The same breakdown occurred in the financial markets. If Wall Street will do anything to sell me an investment, why shouldn't I do whatever it takes to get a loan?

Baza now realized that to fix the housing market over the long term, big changes had to happen all the way up and down the value chain—from the borrowers to the lenders and real estate agents to the regulators.

Wishful thinking obscured reality. Borrowers were allowed—in truth, pushed—to take out wacky mortgages and buy with zero down based on the pipe dream that "house values will always go up."

When they walked away from their mortgages because home prices were declining, they only completed the cycle of irresponsibility.

Abetting it all was the culture of instant gratification that took hold in the U.S. After several decades of economic growth and steadily rising standards of living, prosperity morphed into entitlement, overconsumption, and greed. In 1950, the average household size was 3.4 persons and the typical new house was less than 1,000 square feet. Today, based on the averages, home designers and builders judge that it takes more than 2,500 square feet to house 2.59 people. The double master suite is just one indicator of our times.

At the peak of the housing boom in 2005, Baza remembered his father asking him, "Does someone truly own a house when they put nothing down?" At the time, he had said of course and dismissed his father's reservations as a remnant from the older generation that had no place in today's world. As he sat there listening to the executives testifying, his palms sweating, he so wished he had listened to him more closely.

Baza thought he had found Trina the perfect apartment. It was a small one-bedroom, nothing too splashy, but it was in a new development just south of Houston Street where there was a boatload of gentrification in the works. What had, in the '90s, been a no man's land of crack and crime-infested streets interspersed with the odd after-hours club was beginning to get a facelift. He had texted her to meet him there at 1 p.m. that day.

The subpoenas from the SEC, the FBI and the US Congress had come over the past couple of days. Now the rating agencies were under intense scrutiny. Baza had got caught in a long meeting with Fielding and Jordoin as they were hunkering down and prepping for the hearings and discussing strategies. The last thing Baza should have been doing was leaving the office in the middle of the day, to help his TS paramour no less, (he still wasn't sure what to call her), buy a property and cash in on the boom before it crashed and took him with it.

Nevertheless, he told the pair he simply had to get into see his dentist to deal with an intensely painful tooth and promised to be back within a couple of hours. They looked up at him with blank expressions and Dana said flatly, "Fine. Good luck," and bent her head back over the spreadsheets.

Baza reminded himself that Moody's had been through this before, after the Enron scandal. This was shaping up to be much worse, however, given the major financial meltdown that seemed to be in the making.

Baza's team had been reduced to only thirty people. The flow of new MBS issues had slowed to a trickle, with a collateral reduction in analytical work. The group was now busy full time compiling information in response to the subpoenas. The full scope of their misdeeds and sloppiness would now be out in the open for all the world to see.

In the past, Fielding had dropped into Baza's office once a month or so. Now she came by three or four times a day, asking for this file or that email. The firm had delivered more than 80,000 files to the Justice Department, putting hands every email that had ever been written at Moody's into the government's hands.

On the elevator ride down, Baza was kicking himself for using his Moody's email account for personal matters, such as messages directed to LegsToDieFor@hotmail.com. He knew his files contained dozens, if not hundreds of emails that were personal in utterly damning ways. Among them were several long exchanges with Trina about the Third Sex, as well as numerous articles and pieces of research she had sent him on the topic. Any investigator intent on sniffing out fraud would instantly seize on those emails, seeing them as the smoke indicating an out-of-control fire. Then again, was that anything to really worry about in comparison to what he was about to do? He chuckled to himself out loud at the absurdity of it all and once again felt the heady cocktail of thrill and dread course through his veins.

He figured the inevitable progression of events would be that his condo would be raided, his colleagues and friends questioned—he could already envision Trina's expertly made-up face and shapely legs splashed all over the tabloids and cable news shows. All of his dark secrets would be bared in the harsh light of day.

In the meantime, he hopped on the 6 train and headed downtown to meet Trina and the eager young realtor, Tom Bedford, outside the property on Elizabeth Street, just west of the Bowery. After what felt like an interminably long ride he finally rounded the corner and caught sight of Trina and Tom chatting outside the building. She was wearing a tight short skirt, a jean jacket, and big gold hoop earrings, her hair pulled back into a high ponytail. Baza could only imagine what the realtor must have thought was going on here.

Trina looked nervous and out of her element. Baza approached with a broad smile, feigning a level of confidence he didn't usually feel, and extended his hand to shake Tom's.

"Hi, Mr. Ponce, good to meet you. Why don't you guys follow me?" The realtor led the way into the building and into the sumptuous, mirrored elevator. The interior of the building still had a smell of newness—fresh paint and gleaming marble floors.

"The condos in this building have all just come on and they're already going quickly." Tom's shoes clicked down the hall and he let them into the third-floor apartment with views of the street below. Trina gasped as she walked around the place. It was kitted out with the latest in German engineering—Bosch appliances—and Italian design.

"Oh my God..." she said, trailing her hand along the marble countertops in the small kitchen.

Baza clapped his hands together. "Perfect! What do you think, Trina?" He winked back at Tom, who he had already clocked as being as gay as the night is long. He figured the situation might not arouse even a raised eyebrow from him. He felt reassured by Tom's response.

"I just knew you guys would love this one! I can put forward an offer this afternoon if you two want to have a chat about it." He then busied himself with his phone while Baza and Trina took one more lap around the apartment, looking into all the neatly crafted extra storage spaces that belied the actual square footage of the unit. The architects had definitely been creative in their use of space and Baza knew this would be a huge step up for Trina, who seemed mostly speechless at the moment.

"Does this work for you?" he asked her as they stood looking out the bedroom window onto Elizabeth Street below.

"Yeah, it's gorgeous, Baza, but I don't know how—" Baza put up his hand to stop her.

"As I said, leave it to me. I have some mortgage broker buddies I'll talk to and we'll get you approved for a loan." He walked back out to where Tom was now talking on the phone. He indicated to him that he would call him later and they let themselves out of the apartment while the realtor stayed to either lock up or wait for his next appointment.

Baza intended to call him once he got back to the office and put in an offer for Trina, then call his buddy, Nikos, who had handled his mortgage for his townhouse and see what he could work out. If he was going to go down, it might as well be in a ball of flames as long as he didn't take her with him.

Things came to a head a couple of days later when Baza was called down to Dana Fielding's office. It was right after the announcement had been made to the team that he and twenty-two other Moody's executives were asked to meet with federal investigators. His appointment was set for one week later. He was scheduled to meet with Moody's legal counsel in the interim. The email notice helpfully pointed out, "You, of course, have the option of engaging outside counsel, the costs of which will not be reimbursed by the firm."

He had assumed the meeting was meant to debrief him ahead of the meeting with the federal investigators. He had intended to ask Fielding if she was planning on getting her own attorney, too. When he got to her office things took a different turn. She was sitting with her back to him staring out at the East River.

"Hi, Dana," Baza took his usual seat at the desk and expected her to turn around. She sat there a full two minutes before responding. Finally, she turned around. Her face was ashen and Baza assumed the stress of everything had already taken its toll. She pulled a large manila envelope out of her desk and pushed it across to him.

"What's this?" he asked, suddenly alarmed. He was pretty sure manila envelopes were never a good sign. His worst fears were about to be realized. He could only imagine the photos of him and Trina, as well as other earlier TS prostitutes, all over the cover of the New York Post and Page 3: "Wall Street Financier Caught in TS Scandal."

Baza opened it and, somewhat dazed, pulled out a sheath of papers.

"If you could look at these proposed models as part of Moody's revised positions, I'd really appreciate it, Baza," Dana Fielding said. "I'd appreciate your input before the hearings."

Baza noticed he had stopped breathing for a few seconds. He let a gasp of air go, which came out as a cross between a laugh and a gurgle.

"Yes, of course!" he smiled.

"You okay?" she looked at him curiously.

"Yeah of course, just fine. I think this is a good move."

"Great, you can take those with you. Just get back to me by the end of the day. I need to take this call, excuse me." Dana nodded to the flashing light on her desk phone and picked it up.

Baza took the envelope and managed to get his legs working enough to walk himself out the door and to the bathroom, where he splashed cold water on his face for several minutes before returning to his desk to look at the projections.

Once back to his office, he decided to call one of his former Dartmouth classmates who had gone on to Stanford Law School and was now practicing securities law in San Francisco. He had been retained by a number of dot-com defendants targeted in SEC investigations. He may have dodged this first bullet, but he was still convinced the gun was loaded and there was another one with his name on it not far behind.

"Baza, my man, how goes it in the Big Apple?" Baza found the voice of his old friend, Ted Lindsey, familiar and reassuring in its enthusiasm. Ted was an optimist by nature, a trait that helped him be supportive and helpful to clients who, like Baza, came to him in a daze, knowing their good life was about to end regardless of whether they were proven innocent or guilty.

"Hey, congrats on making partner, Ted. But there's another reason for my call. Things at Moody's are crashing down all around me and I could really use some expert advice.

After hearing Baza's rundown on the situation, Ted said in a reassuring tone of voice, "What are you worried about? You didn't do anything wrong, did you? You guessed the housing market would continue to go up. If that is a crime, then the feds will have to put seventy-five million homeowners in jail."

Baza figured any legal advice from Ted would be worth hearing. He allowed himself to feel momentarily reassured, but it dissolved when he heard Ted's next remark.

"...At the same time, you are smart to be realistic. The feds are under a lot of political pressure, and they will be looking for whipping boys. If they want you, they will get you."

Baza felt as though a lead weight had dropped down into the pit of his stomach.

"...How are you holding up, by the way? You sound terrible."

"That is a perfect word to describe how I am doing," said Baza. Ted's words kept looping through his head, "If they want you, they will get you."

"Here's a suggestion," Ted replied. "Come out to California. I'll gather a small legal team to hear the details of your story and recommend a strategy. Email me the subpoena and anything else you can today. We'll get on it right away.

"Besides, getting out of the line of fire is always a good move. If you fly out tomorrow, we can get together on Saturday. Then you can take a break from Wall Street for a few days, maybe do some hiking over in Marin County. I also promise not to let Lisa organize any blind dates... What do you say?"

At that moment, Baza was grateful for someone who would tell him what to do. /I'll book the tickets right now," he said, feeling the heavy weight on his psyche lifting ever so slightly.

For the last two weeks, he had thought about getting out of town—maybe even running away. Why not walk away, just like all those borrowers who were abandoning their homes and mortgages.

Just get out of town, change your identity, become a bartender—whatever. Just run!

Bill Marshall, a friend of his at NYU, once told the story of how his father had disappeared while the family was living in a small western Indiana farm town. Bill was only ten years old at the time.

"He was a salesman for a sewing machine company, and we knew he was having a hard time making a go of it. But we woke up one morning to find his suitcase, a few clothes and our Chrysler New Yorker were gone. No note, no phone calls, he just left," Bill had recalled, the pain of it still visible on his face.

Years later, Bill got a call from his father. Reluctantly, he went to meet him and hear the reasons why he had abandoned his family. The strong, good-looking father he remembered had turned into a white-haired, weather-beaten old man full of regrets. Bill could still recount every detail of the conversation, as though he had it on tape.

"I was overwhelmed and scared...yes, I was a coward. I got in that old Chrysler, drove north to Interstate 80 and didn't stop driving until I was nearly out of gas. So I filled the tank and kept driving until I was out of gas again. By that time, I was near the western border of Iowa. I didn't stop driving until I got to California and hit the Pacific Ocean. If there had been a bridge to China, I would have kept on going." He had laughed at that, but Bill hadn't seen the humor in it.

"I was in a daze, not able to think. I didn't question what I'd done, and had no clue where I was going—no sir, no sort of plan at all. I think I was having a nervous breakdown right there on the freeway. My life was out of control and I had no way to change it.

"Many times I had the impulse to turn around and go back, but was too ashamed. I realized that from then on, I would always live in shame. It was only right and fitting for someone like me: a coward who was abandoning his family.

"By that point, there was no turning back. I had descended into a place so dark, I couldn't even have imagined it before. It was like being caught in a nightmare and not being able to wake up. I felt this was my fate."

Baza remembered Bill's expression hardening as he told the story. "I don't know...to me he just seemed like some kind of lunatic. He wanted forgiveness and understanding, but I couldn't go there. I didn't pity him, either. He was a coward, all right, and I didn't want anything to do with him. I never saw him again."

Baza thought of Bill's father now—identified with him, in fact. Get on Interstate 80 and don't stop. To him, that sounded like relief. Sure, it was cowardly. But sometimes there's nothing else to do but run away from what you can no longer stand.

There was another way out, of course—the final one. The idea of taking his own life had crossed Baza's mind more than once. His latest suicide fantasy was to take a single step into the path of a Fifth Avenue bus. But as he'd once read, suicide was a permanent solution to a temporary problem.

He'd had another idea, too: He could find a comfortable one-room cabin in a remote wooded location. If he cashed out his 401(k) and his stocks and put all the money into the bank, it would throw off enough interest to pay for food, utilities, a satellite internet connection and all the booze he could drink.

Maybe there'd be a lodge nearby, or a bar where he could go whenever he craved human contact. And a small town with a good coffee shop where he could sit and read the newspaper. That was all he needed.

But this plan also had an end game: To immerse himself in this bucolic environment and slowly drink himself to death.

14

Baza texted Big Bird and asked to meet him at Red's Pub around the corner from Moody's.

"C u in 10," came the instant reply.

Baza arrived first, found a stool in the corner and ordered a Stella Artois. He was nervous and sad about saying good-bye, not only to Big Bird, but to the life he'd had in New York.

Within minutes, Big Bird strutted in with a big grin, just as he had when they first met almost two years ago.

"Ditto on the Stella." Big Bird gulped his beer while Baza sipped.

Skipping any small talk, Baza got right to the point. "About the other day—"

"Forget it, pal. We're all under a lot of pressure and I was out of line." Big Bird tipped his beer bottle towards Baza.

"Good. I agree. I just wanted to tell you, I'm going to California this weekend. Fielding doesn't know this, but I may resign and stay out there while this controversy blows over.

"I wanted you to know how grateful I am for your friendship and the doors you opened to the opportunity at Moody's. I am not sure I did much with it, but I'm grateful for it," said Baza, his eyes downcast as he girded himself for the reaction.

Big Bird jerked his head back as if he had heard that someone close to him had died.

"Listen, Baz, I'll be honest with you. I don't know how all this shit is going to come down in the end, but one thing I do know: we're going to be all right." Big Bird said. "Don't run away, man. This will all work out, I promise!"

"Thanks man, but I don't think it will," Baza replied.

"Listen, you know and I know you were right all along. It's not your fault the rest of us didn't want to hear it. We all wanted to make our numbers much more than we wanted the truth.

"You and I were on opposite sides of a tractor pull, but it was an uneven match. I had the decision-makers and the customers on my side. You had your convictions and an obsolete model that no one wanted to change because it was generating so much money. What is that thing Norman says? 'There is a right way to do wrong.' We didn't do it. But that's our fault, not yours.

"You and me, Baza, we're *simpatico*. We have an understanding. And it's like this. When the dark angels of ill-fortune come into your life, you can't hide from them or wish them away. There is nothing you can do but roll with it until things get better. Even then, the dark angels never really go away; they're always lurking somewhere around the corner. Running from them changes nothing. They'll still be there wherever you go." Big Bird laid his hands on the table for theatrical emphasis before continuing.

"Now I'm going to tell you a story that happened in the place where I grew up," Big Bird said gravely.

"On December 21, 1968, a plumber from St. Louis, a man named Sherman Kline, walked into the second-floor office of the Illinois Department of Child and Family Services at the west end of the Carlinville town square and opened fire on a children's Christmas party. Seven of his ten children were there because they had been taken into the state's foster care system. Three of his children were not in attendance because they had already been adopted into other homes.

"With two .25 caliber pistols, he shot his wife Lorraine, two social workers, Bonnie Albrecht and Frank Wildgrube, a receptionist, and four of his children. Afterward, he drove to a field in O'Fallon, Missouri and shot himself in the head. He died, as did his wife, the two social workers and the receptionist.

"Why did he do it? Because he blamed the government for getting between him and his kids.

"I was in class at Carlinville High when the killings were announced over the intercom. It was right after lunch, I remember, about 2 p.m. We kids were all shocked, but we got to go early. That evening on the CBS Evening News, we watched Walter Cronkite report the story at the very end of his news hour. He showed a map of the United States with a little pin to show where Carlinville was. We went back to school the next day. No therapists ever showed up.

"There were some dark angels hanging around that week, I can tell you," Big Bird said with a far-off look on his face.

Baza wasn't sure exactly what point Big Bird was trying to make.

"Okay, here's the last story I'm going to tell you today. It's about my father—everybody called him Jimmy.

"It happened back in 1940, when he was 19 years old. His grandmother had never learned how to drive, so he would always drive her wherever she wanted to go. The family had a 1938 Ford Deluxe, a real beauty.

"One day his grandmother asked him to drive her and a friend to St. Louis. He was known as a careful driver. But as they approached the turn onto Route 4, a speeding car plowed right through the intersection without even slowing down. It was a horrific crash. The three people in the other car died, and his grandmother was crippled for life. His grandmother's friend was injured, but not seriously.

"When the police came, they arrested my father and later filed manslaughter charges against him. He was eventually found innocent, but the trauma of it almost wrecked the family.

"My aunts and uncles always said that as my dad was growing up, he had been the one to joke and laugh…the life of the party. But by the time I came along—well, I never knew him to smile very often."

Big Bird looked straight into Baza's eyes. "I know where my dark side comes from," he said quietly. "What about yours, my friend?"

Baza hesitated for a moment, then laid down $50 for their beers, rose quickly and reached around to give Big Bird a hug. He felt dwarfed by this bear of a man who had proved to be his friend after all. Neither man said a word, but Baza felt the sting of tears welling up in his eyes.

"Don't do anything stupid," Big Bird said fondly, clasping Baza's hand. "Promise?"

Baza smiled and walked out into the night.

Baza logged onto Expedia and found a JetBlue flight to San Francisco. He thought fondly of Mick, who had since retired from his job presiding over the Big Four Bar, and of the North Beach Restaurant, where he knew the waiters by name and loved the veal saltimbocca. Until now, he hadn't realized how carefree and easy those days really were.

As he reflected on all the crazy times he'd spent in the Big Four, his thoughts drifted to Helen Sharp, a woman he'd met there. Their encounter over a few drinks had turned into an idyllic weekend in Sausalito.

Helen was a 40-something blonde, divorced, with perfectly rounded breasts. She also had sharply protruding nipples, which she liked to show off by wearing fine-gauge sweaters and filmy tops. "Yes, I do have perfect tits," she liked to say, half-kidding, but half-bragging, too.

Baza met Helen at a moment when he was looking for diversion and escape. He had just ended a relationship with a Brazilian banker, Patricia Bustro, whom he had thought he loved, but really didn't. When he said it was over, she had gone berserk and had been making his life miserable ever since. There was a reason that

South American men came to the United States to find women, he thought. One day, he received 100 voice mail messages.

Helen offered the perfect antidote to the Patricia drama.

For four days, Baza hid out in her hillside home on North Street, with its picture-postcard views of the Bay and San Francisco. They drank champagne, ordered in great food from Gourmet Meals on Wheels, leaving the house only once to go have a drink at the Noname a few blocks away in downtown Sausalito. He was still so unnerved about Patricia that he was half-expecting to bump into her.

On the way back, they stopped and rented a bag full of DVDs, including some great porn. They even smoked pot, something Baza had avoided since high school, figuring he was loco enough as it was.

Once past his Patricia paranoia, Baza felt safe that weekend. He even suggested they get a movie with a TS episode in it. It was almost as if he were looking for a way to leak his secret.

"Won't that freak you out?" Helen asked. "Guys are always so weird about that kind of thing."

"Maybe. I'm just curious, she looks so sexy. If the dick part is too strange, we can turn it off," Baza said casually.

"I'm game," Helen laughed.

That long weekend had been years ago, but the memory brought back a wonderful feeling of escape.

After he booked his ticket, he typed "Helen Sharp" into Google, but found no match. A call to directory assistance turned up no one by that name in Sausalito or surrounding communities.

Baza dropped that idea and emailed Dana Fielding to let her know he would be out on Friday.

He added, "FYI: I am meeting with a personal attorney. I just want to get a second opinion about what we might be up against with this investigation. I am happy to share what I learn. I'll be back Monday."

She responded in a matter of minutes: "Stay in touch—this thing seems to be unfolding very quickly. There is an all-day executive meeting on Friday and I may need your input on questions they have for our team. I will be here all weekend."

Fielding was not above guilt-tripping people about the number of hours they put in, but Baza had never been the recipient of those kinds of messages because no one worked more than he did. Of the 75 or so Saturdays since he started at Moody's, he had probably worked 50 and would often bump into Fielding at the office.

Baza booked the flight to California and called Mike Doane, his banker at Merrill Lynch, letting him know that he needed to withdraw at least $5,000 in cash. Doane told him he would raise his daily cash withdrawal limit to $5,000. It was instantly activated and he went downstairs to the Citi ATM near his office and withdrew exactly $5,000.

Next, he crafted an email to his team:

"I will be out of town Friday—in California on family business—and back in the office on Monday. If you need me, call my cell or email; I will check my iPhone for messages. Keep up the good work, and don't worry about what's going on at the company. We can hold our heads high, because you have all consistently done good work."

That night, Baza went to the Ritz-Carlton. Norman was on duty and the crowd was three-deep in front of the bar. When a chair opened up, Norman signaled to Baza, who squeezed into the end seat.

Sitting next to him were three loudmouthed salesmen from the Katz Drug Company in Chicago. They were celebrating their quarterly numbers by drinking and spending as much as they could.

They had bought the entire bar a drink, so Baza now had two martinis sitting in front of him. If he gulped the two drinks, as he usually did when wanting to escape his problems, he would soon begin losing his faculties. Tonight he was determined to avoid trouble, so he nursed the drinks, sipping them slowly over the course of an hour.

He quickly engaged with the three salesmen, who were comparing notes on their recent purchases and acquisitions, each of them trying to top the other. One of the salesmen was boasting to the others that he had single-handedly convinced their CFO to increase their marketing budget by 70% over the past two years and sales of OxyContin were at record high levels. Baza eavesdropped on their conversation a bit longer, shook his head to himself, and wondered how that was going to work out for the company in the long run. After their coffers had been filled, he imagined a country full of zombies on OxyContin stumbling around as they struggled to pay their oversized mortgages. He laughed to himself, marveling that he had any ability to have a sense of humor at this point still. Norman cast him a glance as he was shaking a martini nearby, "You all right there, Baza?"

"Just thinking you're a wise man, Norman. You see it all here, don't you?"

"Yes, I do, indeed I do." They both glanced at the pharma salesman, oblivious in their increasingly drunken celebrations, and laughed.

Of one thing, Baza was certain: Nothing would be the same after this trip. The dark future he pictured ahead was unbearable, but he kept telling himself it wasn't inevitable. He could avoid ridicule and ruin by doing something bold. He would free himself from this torture. He wanted to see Trina before he left but she had some cousins visiting from Hawaii. It did seem that her mortgage had been approved and she was moving ever closer to becoming potentially yet another contestant in the high stakes American drama of homeownership or another victim of this ever propagated myth.

The next morning, his JetBlue flight was an hour late, which only fed his anxiety. As he boarded the plane, he felt momentary relief at leaving the mess behind. But then he imagined being hauled off the plane by the FBI or SEC.

Once he was settled in his seat waiting for takeoff with nothing to do, his imagination began to run amok again. He felt a whole wave of panic attacks poised to engulf him. Sometimes he'd be on the edge of an attack, but it wouldn't materialize. But then the next one was right behind.

He fell asleep on the plane, but woke up several times with the now-familiar cluster of symptoms: heart racing, hands shaking, face was burning up.

He remembered once flying to San Francisco on a first-class Delta flight, sitting next to a troubled father of four sons. His name was Larry Horshing, and he seemed like a decent guy who had gotten himself in some sort of pickle. Baza could tell he was in the grip of a panic attack of some kind. He jabbered for six straight hours, talking around rather than detailing his specific worries. But his agitation was clear. Baza could relate to his pain, so he let him talk on and on.

When they landed, his new friend did not get up, but just sat and stared, face forward, obviously terrified of whatever he was he would face upon getting off the plane.

"Are you OK, Larry?" Baza asked.

"I am just enjoying the last few minutes of this first-class seat. When I was at 37,000 feet I was away from it all and above it all. Now I'm down here. But you can leave me alone, it'll be OK. I just hope your life is working out better than mine."

When Baza crossed through security, his friend Ted Lindsey was waiting with a big smile, holding his four-year-old daughter, Megan, by the hand. She was carrying one of the wholesome-looking American Girl dolls, also named Megan, it turned out, with whom she carried on an animated conversation the entire 45 minutes it took to drive across the Golden Gate Bridge and into Marin County. The Lindsey family lived in the woodsy, but decidedly upscale community of Mill Valley, a place of winding hillside streets, stunning views and endless remodeling.

"You be a good little girl or no ice cream for you tonight. Yes, I know your brother is being mean to you, I will punish him later, while you watch TV," Megan scolded, raising her voice to the doll.

If parents actually took the time to listen when their kids talk to dolls, toys and invisible friends, they would be totally shaken, thought Baza. Kids say things all the time that their parents would consider totally psycho. That's partly because they haven't yet learned to repress their quirks and failings, and partly because they're mirroring the adults they see.

In the 1960s and through the early 1980s, Mill Valley was a haven for rock stars, artists and authors who liked being out of the city, but within easy striking distance. It was also populated by regular folks who liked raising their families among the redwoods and the hiking trails.

Over time, it gradually evolved into an enclave of Rustic Chic. The streets of the small, picturesque downtown were clotted with Range Rovers and Lexus SUVs. Couples pushed $2,000 baby carriages past the funky bookstore and the high-end boutiques. The old drugstore, hardware store and family shoe shop were long gone.

The Lindsey's had a big old restored Craftsman-style house, three acres of land and what appeared to be every gadget in the Williams & Sonoma catalog.

Lisa made dinner and they chatted over expensive red wine until midnight. Baza went to sleep right away, but woke up in the night, sweating profusely. He must have tossed and turned for three or four hours.

He awoke to the noise of Ted making pancakes for Megan.

"Pony up to the bar, partner, you are about ready to taste the best pancakes humankind has ever experienced. I promise you, you are going to write home to your mother in Honduras about them once you have a taste, right, Megan?"

"Where is Hondu.... Hondoor...?" asked Megan.

"Honduras is a small country in Central America," explained Baza.

"Where is Central America?" asked Megan.

"Listen, Baza," said Ted. "I wonder if you could do me a favor. Before we do anything else today, do you mind riding with me up to San Rafael? I'm going to pick up some of your people, day workers, to do some of the digging and clean up around the place. It would be great if you could be my interpreter."

Baza decided to let the 'your people' comment ride and agreed the journey would do him good. Besides, he wanted a chance to talk with Ted on his own.

Ted and Baza drove to the underpass where Highways 101 and 580 converged in San Rafael, which had the largest concentration of Latino immigrants in tony Marin County.

Lined up along Andersen Road were 50 or so illegal immigrant day workers, the very bottom of the Marin County economic pyramid. You could see their desperate yearning for work on their faces and in their body language. Ted, who looked to this labor pool whenever he wanted cheap manual labor, drove into a 7-11 parking lot and spoke in halting Spanish to a couple of solidly built men with deep crow's feet around their eyes. Baza filled in where Ted's Spanish stumbled.

"I need two workers, Mill Valley, eight hours, fifteen dollars," said Ted, enunciating carefully and glancing at Baza.

"*Dos hombres a Mill Valley, ocho horas, quince dólares por hora,*" Baza translated. A self-appointed foreman drifted over and asked for $18 per hour. Ted agreed and two workers jumped into the car, one older and one younger.

Baza heard the younger of the two workers speak, and immediately knew he was Honduran. The man said his name was José.

Baza noticed, that like him, the man was tall for a Honduran. José's features had a more Indian or Mayan cast than Baza's, which reflected his European bloodlines. But at a distance, someone might have taken them for cousins.

Baza asked where in Honduras José was from—"*De donde eres?*"

"Siguatepeque."

It turned out that José recognized the Ponce family name. In fact, he said his uncle had worked on their banana plantation, though it occurred to him it might not be safe to say much more.

At that moment, Baza had what seemed to be a sudden inspiration from nowhere, except it felt more like fate. He had been anxiety-ridden with fear. Now he had a wild idea, an improbable escape plan, and the audacity to believe that he might be able to make it happen. Perhaps he, after all, could be the one to decide how his life would be from now on.

The day workers cut brush and pulled weeds for seven hours in the Lindsey's backyard. Meanwhile, Ted, Baza and the family lazed around the house, drinking mojitos and talking about old times at Dartmouth, the election and what life was like in California.

When the job was more or less done, Baza offered to drive the workers back to San Rafael. Ted was planning to barbecue that evening and hadn't yet picked up the ahi tuna from Whole Foods.

Baza drove north to San Rafael. On the way, he and José chatted easily in Spanish while the older man, tired from the day's work, looked out the window at the sleek automobiles whizzing by. "It must be a hard life being illegal and worrying about the INS," Baza said sympathetically. "Oh no, señor, I am lucky," José replied. "I have a green card. I was here with the illegals because my job building houses was finished. But my family back in Honduras needs the money I send them. I am looking for any work I can get until I find a new job." This gets better and better, Baza thought.

When he dropped the pair off at the 7-11, Baza asked José for his cell phone number, saying that Ted might need more work. José eagerly wrote it down.

On his way back to Ted's, Baza drove past the Mill Valley exit and stopped for a drink at Piatti, a popular hangout next to the Ferrari dealership. It was still early and the bar had not yet filled up. He ordered a double Maker's Mark and ruminated on the plan taking shape in his mind. He'd already labeled it "the switch."

Despite the shred of hope he now felt, he knew the conditions were ripe for a panic attack. He could feel it lurking in the distance, like the chill fog that now hung offshore but would soon cascade over the coastal hills.

Before he left the bar, he checked his email and saw one from Fielding, which he could not bring himself to open.

He drove back to the Lindsey's in Mill Valley and was greeted by the sound of rattling pots and pans and flurry of serious dinner prep. "Honey, would you please bring some fresh cilantro and mint from the garden?" he could hear Ted calling as he walked from the garage toward the kitchen.

Just then, Ted's wife, Lisa, came in the back door carrying a handful of fresh herbs. "Hey, Baza," she said, giving him a hug and a peck on the cheek. "Thanks for helping Ted with the workers today. Come have a glass of wine."

Lisa was a former investment banker, and even after two children and several years away from Wall Street, she hadn't lost her smart, energetic air. Efficient and coolly determined, she mothered, decorated, entertained, volunteered at her children's school, did yoga, and was training for a triathlon. She was the CEO of the smooth-running Lindsey household, not unlike the wealthy

Honduran matriarchs back in his home country, Baza thought. They, too, were good managers, keeping everything in order.

"Do I need a security code for the wireless?" he asked.

"No, anyone and their mother can tap into the Lindsey's wireless. We have no secrets here. Just log right on," said Lisa, who at one point in her career had been Vice President of Business Development for Cisco, the computer hardware company. She knew very well how easily the family's computers could be hacked via an open wireless connection, but she hadn't found the time to install the firewall.

"If you don't mind, I think I will take a nap so I am ready for the party tonight," said Baza.

"Oh sure, go right ahead. I'll try to keep Rusty from barking."

From the guestroom window, Baza looked out over a panorama of wooded hills, million-dollar homes and sailboats still out on San Francisco Bay. The waves reflected flashes of pink, gold and orange in the early evening light. He lay down on the crisp white damask comforter and closed his eyes. He was asleep within minutes.

Baza logged onto his laptop, opened the email from Fielding.

The attachment was a letter informing Baza that he had been let go. It explained that the firm was being restructured and Fielding's entire group, including Baza's analytical team, was to be reorganized.

Baza reread the letter. It was written by the HR legal team and included one particularly chilling sentence, "The firm is no longer in a position to represent you in any pending or future legal matters that you face."

Earlier, Baza had found it difficult to get a clear cell phone signal in this part of Marin County, but suddenly the message icon appeared on his phone. Calling voicemail, he retrieved messages from Fielding, Kaplan, Sandra and two unknown numbers. He also had a message from his father in Honduras.

Baza stood up, unsure of what to do. His heart began to race. He wanted a drink, a cigarette and a hooker. Feeling an overwhelming urge to move, he needed some time to get his bearings before facing the evening's nonstop gourmandizing.

Skirting the backyard, he slipped out the side entrance to the house, walked to the gate at the end of the fence, and fumbled with the latch, stumbling around like an intruder.

Huffing a bit, Baza took rapid, shallow breaths as he walked quickly to the street. The San Francisco fog had now moved in, engulfing the streets at lower elevations. The wet mist hit his face. It would have felt bracing, except he was having trouble getting his breath.

He stopped and sat on the curb behind a big black Mercedes. The streets were lined with SUVs, BMWs and one Toyota Hybrid. Up here in the hills, the homes sprawled across the ridgelines, with expansive decks and plots of lush green grass that had replaced the native scrub and live oaks. Nearly all had been remodeled from top to bottom; occasionally, one would see a brand-new house spring up where someone had bought a tear-down. The yards were perfectly manicured, the big trees were trimmed and the driveways had few cracks.

He thought of this scene being replicated in metropolitan areas all across the country. There was so much waste...so much excess and greed—and for what? Baza felt confusion. What did he really aspire to here in the United States? Why had he been so easily lured by the quick wealth to be made in the credit rating business?

Walking slowly down the dusty shoulder of the Lindsey's hillside street, he was suddenly struck by the fear that the feds had probably been alerted that he was in California. Moreover, they might be coming to arrest him right now! As he saw car headlights approaching, he ducked behind a tree.

He reached into his pocket for his iPhone and called Dana Fielding on her home number. It was about 8 p.m. in New York. His former boss picked up the call, probably while stroking her cat.

"Baza, hi! How are you?" she began in an artificially bright tone. "I'm glad you called. I wanted to apologize for delivering the news by email, but Legal required it. My hands were tied.

"Here's the thing you must realize: You failed miserably. You are a disgrace to this company. I will personally see that you rot in jail," Fielding said.

"Right. One question, though. Why couldn't this have waited until my return on Monday?" he asked.

Baza heard a sharp click. Fielding had already hung up.

Sweating profusely, Baza awoke from his nap with a throbbing headache and the feeling that everything had gone wrong while he was sleeping.

Now he remembered: He was fired. Officially disgraced. Wasn't he? His thoughts were muddled; his hold on reality felt slippery. Was this what it was like to be crazy?

.He glanced around the room at the watercolor landscapes that hung on the walls, waiting as his life slowly booted up before him.

He reached for his cell phone to check the time; he had slept a good 90 minutes. God, could it have been a dream? Was there really an email? If so, what was in it? He was flooded by relief, confusion and dread, all at once.

Baza held his breath as Outlook listed his newest emails. His heart sank as he saw there was indeed an email from Moody's. Perhaps the truth was even worse than he had imagined.

He clicked on it, blinking when he saw a brief, blandly worded message exhorting him to "please carefully read the enclosed pdf." He felt as though he was trying to run underwater.

To his amazement, the attachment turned out to be a lengthy document, in small type, pertaining to legal counsel and the federal inquiry of Moody's. In stilted legalese, it notified him of the limits to the company's obligation to represent him; it also outlined the requirements that he disclose all pertinent information to the firm. He was to affix his electronic signature and return it to the firm within 24 hours.

He sat on the bed, limp, as the sweat evaporated from his skin, leaving a salty, slightly sticky residue.

The document from Moody's was not the termination memo he had expected and dreamt about, but a standard cover-your-ass agreement designed to help the firm demonstrate that it wasn't hiding anything. He laughed out loud, not sure if he was more relieved or more horrified—suddenly feeling like being fired would have been preferable to the prospect of public humiliation, and even potential imprisonment, that lay before him. Under other conditions, being fired would have spun him out of control. But he realized this fate would be preferable to remaining. It was all too easy to picture his personal life displayed in lurid details for all eyes to see.

Since Watergate, cover-ups had become the crime most likely to bring down high-profile business executives or politicians. With enough expensive legal talent, they could often beat the rap for the original crime based on theatrics before a jury or some obscure technicality.

But if they were caught in a lie—bingo! It wasn't hard to make a perjury charge stick. Just ask Martha Stewart.

Any company found to be complicit in these lies is also vulnerable to prosecution, as Arthur Andersen, the accountants for Enron, soon learned. Their role in keeping Enron's activities under wraps brought about the collapse of the entire firm.

For the moment, Baza still had his job. But the feds were circling, sniffing Moody's up and down, and he was undeniably at the heart of the trouble. It was only a matter of time. The bad dream and the reality were bound to converge.

Baza stood up and circled the room. He looked out the window and saw Megan playing in the yard with Josefina, another in her collection of American Girl dolls. The little girl had this doll, suited up in a homemade cape and other supergirl accouterments, going after people who weren't nice to cats.

This made Baza wonder, as he had many times before, about the prospects for a country so prosperous that people fussed over the comfort of their pets while ignoring human misery and poverty all around them. He remembered being at a dinner party, a few weeks before, where two successful lawyers were exchanging views on what constituted the number-one issue of the day. Regina, a partner in one of New York's top intellectual-property firms, had insisted it was animal rights.

Now that Baza was fully awake and in greater command of his faculties, he decided he was definitely disappointed that his position had not been terminated. That would at least have given him an understandable excuse for slipping into oblivion and leaving his team out to dry.

He became more resolute about his plan, and upon reflection decided that it was a good one—maybe even brilliant. Yes, it was cowardly; that he could admit. But events were unfolding in a way that compelled him to reach for the escape hatch.

His plan was simple: he would buy José's identity. The man named Baza Ponce would simply disappear.

He would forget New York, give up his accumulation of possessions, and become a free man. Maybe he would wander across the country for a while, leading a simple, nomadic existence until he figured out his next steps. Or, he would find a place to hide out in the redwood country north of here.

Sonoma, Lake and Mendocino Counties were ideal places to hide out. People there did not ask questions, for one simple reason: They did not want anyone asking them questions.

Baza used his cell phone to call José and arrange a meeting for the next morning in San Rafael. Next, he asked Ted for the use of one of the family's several vehicles to visit a friend in the city. Lisa told him he was welcome to take the Toyota Highlander the children's nanny used during the week.

Ted and Lisa had invited a dozen or more people to the party that evening. One of the guests turned out to be one of Baza's old drinking buddies from Lucky Cheng's in New York. Tommy Hart was a 72-year-old San Francisco lawyer who had represented some notorious characters in the 1960s, including Charles Manson, which did not make him too many friends, but did gain him considerable notoriety. He showed up at the party with his girlfriend, a news anchor on one of the local TV stations, who looked to be roughly half his age.

Tommy had a knack for living life to its fullest. In the early 1970s, he had bought a 160-acre ranch in western Sonoma County. The property was high on a hill at the end of a treacherous, one-lane dirt road that took 45 minutes to traverse. If you didn't have an all-wheel-drive vehicle, you couldn't get there at all.

At the very top of the hill was a party house with a pool, a long, well-stocked bar and a dance floor. Nearby were multiple guest houses that Tommy had also built. In his younger years, he was famous for hosting blow-out parties. Baza never got tired of hearing stories about the days and nights of revelry up on Tommy's mountain. They spoke of freedom from interference, and of escape with no consequences—the two things Baza had always thought he wanted most in life.

Now, nursing his wine and picking at the extravagant buffet Ted and Lisa had put out, Tommy looked enervated, almost frail. With some help from Ted's firm, he had just wound up a case in which he successfully defended a prominent doctor accused of receiving child porn on his computer. The investigation, which had started with child porn, also turned up evidence of Medicare fraud, an area in which Ted's firm was expert.

"What a messy case it was," exclaimed Ted. "It also showed how far the government could go, given half an excuse, in probing everything about our lives. If they want you badly enough, they'll find a way to make your life miserable."

The color left Baza's face. He wanted to end this conversation. "Can I get you another glass of wine, Tommy?" he said weakly.

Tommy shook his head and Baza walked away, anxious to find a cocktail and attempt to quell his latest batch of anxieties.

If they want you, they will get you.

Baza fought to tame his fears with logic and analytical thinking. "Think, Baza," he told himself. "Worst case...what is the worst case?"

The feds could accuse him of tampering with Moody's model... or not tampering with the model, depending on whatever twisted accusation they could come up with. They would discover he was friends with Big Bird, and would assume he had taken kickbacks to compromise analyses—which he hadn't. They would find out about their trip to Vegas and other assorted meet-ups with clients, bankers and brokers.

The company did not have a strict policy on this kind of mingling, but it didn't look good in the context of things. Wasn't Moody's guilty of duping investors into pouring way too much capital into the housing market and causing what could become a major financial meltdown? Wasn't that some sort of crime?

One thing was certain. Between the federal government investigations and the press, Baza was destined for humiliation, if not jail. And Moody's would be pulling strings behind his back with their portfolio of his transgressions with TS hookers and porn.

If they want you, they will get you.

He had just read a review of a new book called *Three Felonies a Day: How the Feds Target the Innocent* by attorney Harry Silvergate, who decried federal prosecutors run amok. This confirmed more of his worst fears.

On occasion, when he was not overstressed at work, was exercising regularly, and was staying away from alcohol, Baza would have moments of clarity about his fears and how divorced they were from reality. At those times, he would find a grip on sanity once again. But his freedom from irrational fear would only last until his next binge.

15

As he sat and pondered his plan, he recalled a panic attack that had occurred almost two decades before.

In his first year at Dartmouth, he was sure that he was going to get into trouble over the activities of his roommate, Mark Gleason, who made and sold fake driver's licenses. Though Baza was in no way connected with the scheme, he imagined a scenario in which he would be implicated.

He became so convinced disaster was imminent that, for months, he avoided driving his car. He was afraid that if he was pulled over for a routine traffic violation, he would somehow be traced to Gleason's operation and busted for a massive conspiracy to defraud the federal government.

His panic attack was, as always, a considerable distance from the truth. He finally got over his imagined vulnerability when his father visited Hanover and Baza escorted him all over town without being taken into police custody.

The way he found sanity was by concocting an irrational response to his irrational fears. The narrative was of his own making, so he invented it as he lived it. His phone vibrated in his front pocket. He took it out and read a text from Trina.

Closing on the condo next week. I'm so grateful for all you've done for me. Xoxo

He felt a pang in his chest as he realized that in the midst of all his own self-absorbed anxiety, he hadn't talked to her in several days to find out how the sale was progressing. Now he had dragged Trina into this mess too. Was he prepared to disappear on her with no explanation?

Before his brain had time to stop his finger, he had hit the call button on his phone and heard her number ringing.

"Well hello, baby," she drawled.

"Hey, I'm traveling for work now. I just wanted to…say hi. When are you closing?"

"Friday next week," she answered. "You back by then?"

"Uh…yeah, I should be. I mean why wouldn't I be?"

"All right mystery man, we'll have to have a little celebration when you return."

"That would be nice," Baza said, unsure how to proceed. He knew what he really wanted to say wouldn't be fair to her. He wanted to say *are you sure you really want to do this? It may be the worst decision you've ever made and it's all my fault.* Instead he said, "I'll call you next week," and hung up.

Baza got up early on Sunday, had a cappuccino with Ted at the Depot in downtown Mill Valley, and then drove up to San Rafael to meet José. Ted was still putting together a legal team for a session with Baza at his office the next day.

Mt. Tamalpais was perfectly framed in the blue California sky by the bold white contrail of an eastbound jet passing overhead. Baza wondered how many souls on that plane were running away from some mess.

When Baza pulled up, José was conversing animatedly with another immigrant, who had already been waiting two hours in hopes of work that day. José was wearing the same plaid flannel shirt, blue jeans and Oakland A's baseball cap he'd worn the previous day. He greeted Baza with a nod and a shy smile. As he climbed into the car, he looked briefly over his shoulder, which he seemed to do frequently.

Baza got onto Highway 101 and headed north, in the opposite direction from Mill Valley. José gave him a quizzical glance, but said nothing. Baza clicked on the radio, tuning in to a Spanish station that was playing Hector Lavoe. José knew the song and hummed along under his breath.

"We're not going to Mill Valley today," Baza told his countryman in Spanish. "We are driving about an hour north to a small town called Cazadero in Sonoma County. I am considering buying *uno pequeño escondite*, a small cabin, up there. I would like you to help me figure out what it will take to get the grounds in shape and maintain them. I will pay you the same as you got yesterday, $18 an hour. *¿Está de acuerdo?*"

José nodded agreement, but continued to stare ahead.

Looking at available properties on Realtor.com, Baza had found an unusual hideaway, a one-room cabin in an isolated redwood grove off Kidd Creed Road. It took only a few minutes on Google Earth to determine that there were no other houses anywhere within a quarter-mile of this secret lair.

The description sounded almost too good to be true. "One-room retreat, cleaned up by current owner; includes Internet/Satellite TV. Private lane, three acres, complete privacy. Some legal issues."

It occurred to Baza that "legal issues" might be advantageous to him—or not. Either way, it certainly explained the below-market price.

On the way north, they discussed Jose's family, his immigration papers, where he worked and how he sent money back home each month. Baza was careful not to gloat about his family's position in Honduras; they talked about fishing, mountains and ocean spots that they both knew. By the time they approached Cazadero, they had even shared how much both men had missed their families back home.

As they drove, the temperature rose into the high seventies. But the instant they turned toward the coast and into the redwoods, it cooled down. Baza put on the vivid orange microfleece pullover he'd packed, knowing it was such generic northern California garb that he'd blend right in.

A local real estate agent, 62-year-old Bill O'Toole, was waiting for them when they arrived at the gate to the cabin. He smiled and waved them in. A short, compactly-built man of Irish descent, O'Toole seemed like he had been transported directly from Boston's South Shore to this Redwood outpost. Baza quickly learned that despite his demeanor, O'Toole had lived and worked for more than 30 years in the western part of Sonoma County—the funky side of Sonoma Valley, the Irishman clarified. He explained how the area's ambiance came in part from the towering redwoods and the rough-hewn, low-rise storefronts in the small towns that dot the edge of the river.

As Baza and Jose walked around the grounds, Bill continued to narrate a history of the area, as if reciting his normal purchase pitch.

"You know, in the sixties, west Sonoma was full of hippies, with their dope patches and organic farms. In the seventies, gays discovered the area, which was isolated enough to seem exclusive, yet close enough to the Bay Area to be practical."

"Uh-huh," Baza offered little in the way of encouragement for Bill's loquacity.

"They added a certain element of gentrification and economic stimulus and even the locals were pleased to see more remodeling jobs and better restaurants cropping up. Yuppies mostly went elsewhere—they preferred the town of Sonoma and Napa Valley to the east.

Bill was the perfect agent for Baza, as he seemed totally uninterested in the background of the two Hondurans and asked no questions about where they were from or why they wanted to move to Sonoma. They could have been brothers, lovers, drug dealers or pimps for all O'Toole seemed to care.

His narrative then took a more reflective turn.

"As if the news about Iraq and the economy weren't enough, the items from the Bay Area make it sound like mayhem down there, with all the road warriors commuting to and from work," said O'Toole, shaking his head. "I can't tell you how glad I am not to be part of that."

"Yeah, I know what you mean," said Baza. He said nothing about being from New York.

Baza loved the property, and the price was right—just $110,000, a pittance in this part of the world. It was a one-room redwood cabin that sat right on Kidd Creek. A rickety walking bridge crossed the creek to the road, where there was a carport just wide enough for one vehicle. The owner had fixed up the place in order to sell it, adding skylights, a wood-burning stove, and a swing out back. The few basic pieces of furniture Baza would need were already there, and the hot water worked.

"I oversaw the improvements for the owner myself," O'Toole informed them.

José looked around with a puzzled expression. Except for a few bushes planted next to the house and some flowers out by the gate, the lot was largely natural and uncultivated. It wouldn't take more than a day's work to clear the few patches of overgrown brush, and yard maintenance would be almost nil.

"*Es muy bonito*—very nice," he said, approvingly.

Baza turned to O'Toole. "Your listing made some reference to legal issues," he said.

"Yes, there is some dispute about access to the property from the bridge to the road, and there is a lien on the property because of downstream water damage resulting from some work the previous owner did on the creek," O'Toole said. "That has prevented a clean sale. It's also the reason the price is far less than this property should command."

"Would the seller consider a lease with an option to buy," asked Baza, "with $10,000 in cash as a down payment?" Baza's motivation for the suggestion was that a lease/option would not be recorded as a transaction, so there would be no public record, but would give the buyer certain legal privileges, such as the ability to limit access by the landlord.

"I am sure the seller would consider such an offer. I can call him this afternoon and get back to you later today, I have your cell number."

"Fine," Baza smiled, eager to be cooperative.

The house was perfect—livable, hidden and private. It was everything Baza had hoped for. The elements of his plan were beginning to come together.

Trying to keep up his ruse for the moment, Baza walked the grounds with José, pointing out areas for clearing or planting, then circled back to O'Toole and reached out to shake his hand, which was as limp as the man was laconic. "Thank you very much. I'll look forward to hearing what the owner says and when I might be able to move in."

He pulled the SUV out onto the road; no other vehicles were in sight except for the occasional logging truck. They traveled down Cazadero Highway to Route 116, then turned west toward the ocean. They could follow Route 1 down the coast before heading back toward civilization.

A warm breeze whipped up, blowing through the valley. The redwoods were shedding low-hanging leaves like a dog losing its fur in spring.

The Pacific was wild along this stretch of coast, with huge waves crashing over the jagged rock formations that rose from the surf. As they passed Bodega Bay, Baza and Jose chatted about the boats they saw moored in the harbor. The silences in between reminded Baza of the secrets he was harboring.

Stopping at a roadside taqueria for lunch, they hungrily ate burritos as they sat on a bench facing the sea. Baza reflected for a moment on the risks of the path he was about to take. Here he was, a member of the privileged class who had been afforded every advantage from birth. Yet the anxieties he felt, due partly to the pressures of being one of the elite, had made his life unbearable. Would a radically simpler lifestyle really provide the refuge he was looking for?

It wasn't as though he had no other choice. For one thing, he could go home to Honduras. His father certainly had enough influence to block extradition, at least for a time, if it came to that.

He could also face up to his crimes, take whatever was coming to him, and move on. His father had always held that dealing with a problem foursquare was the only sensible and honorable course.

"If you try to lie or run away, things invariably get worse," the elder Baza had counseled.

As usual, Baza's moment of clarity—his ability to weigh his options calmly and rationally—crumbled under the weight of his dark impulses and anxieties. Everything in him screamed "run away."

Baza wondered what flaws of neurology or character made it so difficult for him to uphold the family values and virtues that had been preached to him since childhood. He concluded that it did not matter, since he knew no other way to be.

He swallowed the last bite of his burrito, delicately dabbed his paper napkin at his mouth and took a deep breath.

Baza turned toward José and looked him right in the eye. "José, I have something important to ask you...something that could mean a big opportunity and make a big difference in your life." José looked startled and just blinked at Baza as he spoke.

"I need a new start in life, and will pay you $50,000 in cash if you give me your papers and let me take over your identity. I will give you another $5,000 for a car and will help you get a fake passport. You can drive to Honduras through Mexico, be home in two or three weeks and have all the money you need to start a life in your country. Never again will you be at the mercy of the gringos or have to beg anybody for work."

Joséstuck his hands in his pockets and studied the horizon on the sea.

"What do you say?"

Without a word, Jose carefully gathered his trash and deposited it in the container. After a minute, he looked over at Baza.

"*Usted está loco*," he said, repeating "you are *loco*" over and over again.

Baza walked into Moody's offices on Monday morning and felt the eyes follow him across the room, flitting away as he passed each desk in the huge open plan seating area. He half-smiled to himself as he walked into Dana Fielding's office and shut the door behind him, but didn't bother to sit down. She was on the phone and was clearly annoyed to see him invite himself in and interrupt their customary protocol.

"Dan, I'll call you back," she said, replacing the receiver. "Baza, do you mind? I was in the middle of a call."

"Yes, actually I do, Dana, sorry. I just wanted you to hear it from me first. I want you to know I thought about everything you said over the weekend, and I just want to assure you I will comply completely with all the hearings and investigations."

"Well, that's good to hear Baza. I'm sure if we just tell the truth everything will come out fine."

"Right. I'll be taking off the rest of the day to prepare for tomorrow." He turned on his heel and left. He had some calls to make.

His meeting with Ted and his team of lawyers in Mill Valley had given him some new ideas and perspectives on the fight that lay before him. He needed to talk to Big Bird, except this time Baza was calling Sandra into the meeting, too. But it needed to be somewhere different. He knew Sandra liked to go to the driving range at Chelsea Piers when she got off early enough. He called her.

"Hi, it's me," he said, piling files into his briefcase at the same time.

"Baza? Somehow I thought you might not come back from California. I'm so happy you did, just in time for all this shit," she said.

"Yeah listen, I need your help. Can we meet later? Maybe at Chelsea Piers if you're going to hit your driving range? I want Mike to come, too."

"Uh...okay sure, we can do that. Why don't we just meet at Galaxy Diner on 10th Avenue at 6:30. That work?"

"Perfect, see you there." Baza hung up and called Big Bird. He didn't need to announce himself.

"My little Latino friend! I was beginning to wonder about you." Big Bird's voice boomed through the cell phone.

"Listen, I want to talk with you and Sandra," Baza then invited him to also meet at the diner.

"That's the back of beyond, man. I don't go that far west."

"Come on, Mike, this is important. I need to run some things by you before this hearing tomorrow." Baza tried to keep the pleading note out of his voice.

"Okay brother, I'll be there," he said, before clicking off.

Baza finished packing up all of the relevant hard copies of records he could manage to fit inside his soft Italian leather briefcase. He then took an external hard drive out of his gym bag and downloaded everything from his laptop, which belonged to Moody's, and he intended to leave in the office. He didn't want any of their property.

Before leaving, Baza made a few more calls. There were favors to call in and he went down his list meticulously.

First, he phoned Rick Bunting in London. He explained what was happening with the hearings and how Baza felt like he was likely to go down in a ball of flames. Rick's voice was reassuring and he made Baza realize how much his panic and anxiety often got the better of him. Despite Rick's true opinion of the practices that were all in play, he encouraged Baza to stick to the line that he was working with the best information they had available at the time and that he made all of his calls in good faith. Baza didn't see how good faith was going to keep him out of jail, but he tried to take Rick's words to heart.

He rang off, promising Rick an update after the dust had settled. Next he called Kate. He had been putting off talking to her since she was in town for a visit a few weeks earlier and had wanted some kind of answer from Baza on the direction of their relationship.

"Baza, what's wrong?" Kate knew him well enough by now to hear the anxiety in his voice.

"Kate, I'm sorry I haven't been in touch. And I'm sorry I've been a shitty...cxcusc for a boyfriend," he faltered, suddenly feeling presumptuous for even using the term to refer to himself.

"Right," she said, and waited for him to continue. Baza took a deep breath and plunged in, confessing his lifelong confusion about relationships, women, sexual preferences, marriage, family—he left no box unticked. It was like some kind of damn had broken and once he started, he couldn't stop himself. While he didn't mention

Trina specifically, he told her about his explorations into the trans world and he could only imagine her white Protestant toes curling.

"I'm sorry I haven't been honest with you. I really have a tremendous amount of respect and care for you Kate, and you have deserved better. I'm sorry." He finally took a breath and waited.

After about thirty seconds of silence she spoke. "Well, Baza, I actually can't say I'm totally surprised."

"Really?" he was incredulous. "You're not surprised?"

"You're not as good at hiding who you really are as you think," Kate said. "But it's okay. I do appreciate you telling me all this. And honestly, I wish you the best."

"Really?" he said again, realizing he was repeating himself.

"Yes, really, I do. And good luck with the hearings. Goodbye, Baza." She clicked off and the line went dead. Baza felt a bit dazed. The drama and anxiety around airing his secret was not nearly as bad as he had imagined. He wondered if the ramifications of his actions were always worse inside his head. He would have liked to talk to her more, but fair enough, he had said his piece, he couldn't really expect she would want to keep chatting with him as if nothing had changed. He hung up, grabbed his now bulging briefcase and left the building.

In the taxi up the Westside Highway, he made one last phone call: to a reporter at *The New York Times* whose card he had been carrying in his wallet for months. The reporter had interviewed him a while back for a piece about the real estate bubble and at that point he had thoroughly towed the company line. He wanted to offer another perspective, on condition of anonymity, as a parting shot and salve for his conscious concerning his involvement in the whole unfolding debacle.

Baza arrived at the Galaxy Diner, a staple on 10th Avenue for as long as any old-time New Yorkers could remember. Though once the refueling point for the late-night denizens of the hookers and dealers of 10th Avenue, and a daytime haunt for local neighborhood laborers, now it was all polished up new for the frontiersmen gentrifying this western stretch of Manhattan.

He slid into a booth and ordered a Corona from the waitress who sailed by, barely pausing to toss a menu on the table. Within minutes, Sandra arrived. He watched her alighting from a taxi and waved from the window. She joined him in the booth. Just then his phone started blowing up with texts from Trina.

The mortgage adviser just called to say the bank rescinded the offer? WTH Baza? What does this mean??

Never mind he said it means the sale isn't going thru!!

What am I going to do Baza?? You said this would work!!

"Baza, you okay?" Sandra asked, looking genuinely concerned. Baza shoved the phone back into his pocket. He couldn't deal with this now. He should have known. He kicked himself even harder for bringing this on Trina.

"All things considered, I'm stellar," he forced a smile and took another swig of his Corona.

Sandra ordered black coffee just as the door to the diner swung open and Big Bird and his huge presence entered. Simply due to the larger than life air that preceded him, he never failed to turn heads. Big Bird heaved himself into the booth next to Sandra who had to scoot to the wall to leave enough room for his girth. He signaled to the waitress to bring him two Coronas. Baza couldn't help noticing that the Mexican beer hater had changed his tune.

"Speak to me, brother." Big Bird boomed.

"I just want you both to hear it from me, in case I don't get a chance to tell you again, that I take full responsibility for everything—for all of Moody's ratings these past few months."

"What the hell are you talking about?" Big Bird practically barked at him. "We didn't tell anybody to jump off a cliff. We gave our ratings on deals and at the end of the day, they only amount to our opinions—and this was a team effort."

"Mike's right," Sandra said. "It's not like this comes down to individual responsibility, Baza."

"I've decided that for me, it does. I just want you guys, when you get subpoenaed, to say that you advised against these ratings, but I didn't listen and ultimately it was my call."

"Have you lost your mind, buddy? This game isn't about personal responsibility. It's about making money for our clients and the man upstairs and that's what we did." Big Bird drained the first Corona and took a swig of the second one.

"I'm not going to argue with you, but that's what I want you to do for me. Please. Trust me. It's best this way. I'm going to be fine." Baza was feeling calmer and clearer than he had in longer than he could remember. "Sandra, you've been an amazing associate. Thank you so much. I couldn't have gotten through this without you."

"Baza, this is...I mean...crazy. Like, where are you going?" Sandra looked at him skeptically.

He just shrugged. "I don't know. Maybe nowhere. We'll see." He wasn't about to share his plan with them. Though since he got back from Mill Valley, he was feeling less sure about what that was.

"I told you buddy, you've just gotta ride out the storm. It'll all blow over in a few months and it will be business as usual," Big Bird said, gesturing broadly.

"I hear you man, just think of this as me painting a 'what if' scenario in that case," Baza said. "Maybe just lay low for a bit."

"All right, fair enough," Big Bird replied. "But listen man, this is going to be my best year yet. I'm fairly sure it can be the same for you, amigo."

"Okay then, thanks. Listen, I gotta go. You guys take care. Thanks for meeting me." Baza shook both of their hands, which seemed awkward given the informality of the meeting, but somehow it gave him a sense of closure. They both looked bewildered as he then gave them a final wave and left the restaurant.

He walked as briskly as his legs would take him until he got to 8th Avenue and 50th Street, where he ducked down into the subway and waited for the next C train to take him downtown. Baza found himself fantasizing about disappearing into the bowels of Alphabet City, never to be seen again by civilized society. He then thought about the cabin in the woods of Northern California. It came to him in a flash that neither option was right. There was a place he had yearned to explore but had never been. A place that might hold some of the anonymity and beauty of each of these two extremes, but had weather to beat both. First, he had to calm Trina down and see if he couldn't get her out of the mess he'd created for her.

16

The aquamarine blue water lapped the shore as the fisherman pulled in their catch from the day, working in tandem with each other as they gathered their large nets and pulled them aboard their wooden boats. A storm was gathering in the east as the sun was setting, creating beautiful deep violet hues mixed with the burnt orange of the late summer sun. Baza found himself whistling as he wiped down the bar, getting ready for the inevitable happy hour crowds of locals and tourists that would start drifting in soon, smelling of suntan lotion and the sea. He couldn't remember the last time he whistled and suddenly thought to himself that he actually felt like a much younger man.

He looked over at Trina, who was sitting at a table in the corner, drinking coffee as she planned their menu for the week. She wore a beach caftan and her caramel-colored skin enabled her to slip in and look like a local in this off the beaten path outpost on the south coast of Baja, California, close to the Mexican border.

Baza greeted an American couple in their 30s who slid onto the stools at the end of the bar, looking a bit sheepish, as if they hadn't quite gotten into their holiday groove yet and were wondering if 10 a.m. was too early to start drinking. Baza had adopted some of the lingo of the locals and spoke English as if he was not the agile speaker that all his years in the U.S. had afforded him. More than anything, it was a little game he liked playing, if for no one else's benefit than his own. He was enjoying feeling anonymous and blending in and didn't need his pedigree questioned, to be asked what circumstances in life might have landed him behind this bar and not a trading desk in New York, London, or Singapore.

"Hola, amigos, what you like to drink today?" he smiled easily.

The man put up two fingers, as if he wasn't sure his English would be understood. "Two mojitos please, sir."

"Comin' right up. You come to the right place my friends. We make the best mojitos you'll find anywhere in Baja." He winked at them as he set to work crushing the limes. "Where you from?

"New York. We're just here for the weekend. Get away from it all for a bit." The man seemed to be the talker.

"Ah, the Big Apple. Never been myself. Hear it's a crazy place!" Baza chuckled. He let the couple alone as he worked on their cocktails. Over the past several months in their new home he had become a student of cocktail art. He would never have imagined he could have gained so much simple pleasure from creating and sharing a sugary, alcoholic concoction with an artistic flair that took minutes to create and even fewer to consume. Ephemeral, consumable and beneficial. Like a potter that threw pots on the kiln, transforming wet clay into useful objects for the home. Baza likened his new line of work to creating uplifting moments of escapism for his customers.

Being in this serene setting had actually taken the edge off his own drinking compulsion and he found himself imbibing much less than he had in years and feeling more optimistic than ever. So he was careful to cut his customers off when he felt they were at their limit. He saw himself in them too many times. And he didn't need their money. He especially didn't want their broken nose from slamming into the pavement on their way home, or worse, crashed their rental car over a cliff, on his conscience. Escapism, just the right amount, had become his new motto.

Baza looked past his bar patrons at the couple in their 70s reclining on the beach chairs under the large multi-colored umbrella. The man was snoring and the woman was reading the newspaper. He still couldn't quite believe his father had accepted his offer of a week in Baja with himself and Trina. He hadn't spoken to his parents for months. He figured they were happy that he was alive, so they didn't ask any questions about his personal life.

His father's response to Baza leaving everything behind was much less extreme than he could ever have imagined. He realized that all these years he had been so busy trying to please his parents and be a good son, that he had never really even tested the boundaries to see where the confluence of his own personal needs and dreams crossed with his parents. As the eldest son, he had felt compelled to be the example and tow the family line for the next generation of Ponce's. It had never occurred to him to give his parents credit for seeing through some of the excesses of America's current fever of consumption by way of the housing market. They confessed to him they were actually relieved he was out of it all. Of course, he also knew they supposed this current lifestyle was just a recovery period for him and he would go back to being an upstanding member of society who would continue to look after the family fortunes and legacy.

Baza was making no promises, but he was looking forward to sharing some ideas with his father about ways to build their business in Honduras and maybe if he ever got tired of his still-new beach bartender life in Baja, he would move back.

"What do you folks do in the big city?" he asked his customers nonchalantly as he set their mojitos before them and went back to polishing some glasses.

The guy, who wore small wire-rimmed glasses that gave his early balding pate a studious look, glanced at his wife before answering. "Let's just say I was in banking."

"Ah, say no more," Baza smiled and offered the couple a bowl of salted mixed nuts. He found this usually made people drink just a bit more than they normally would. And he sensed this guy had a story to unload, but he would let him do so in his own time. Baza had become a bit of an expert in his new role of behind the bar counselor and confessor. He had a long arm of experience and enjoyed the tables being turned. But there was no hurry. Perhaps he would save another soul this week, perhaps he wouldn't. "How long you folks here for?"

"A week," the wife offered, flipping her long red hair off her shoulders.

"Well, you two kick back and enjoy. We start serving food at 5. Trina here makes a mean Sancocho," Baza said, nodding towards Trina who was making a list for the market.

"What's that?" the woman asked.

"It's like the best chicken stew you've ever tasted. Particularly good hangover cure. Just sayin'." Baza winked at the couple and began slicing limes so he'd have enough for what he anticipated would be a busy day at the Barracuda Tiki Bar.